PRAISE FOR LAURENCE SHAMES' NOVELS

"Characters flashier than a Key West sunset and dialogue tastier than a conch stew."

– New York Times Book Review

"As enjoyable as a day at the beach."

—USA Today

"Funny, suspenseful, romantic, and wise."

—Detroit Free Press

"Smart and consistently entertaining."

—Chicago Tribune Book Review

"Delicious dark humor and healthy cynicism."

' —San Francisco Chronicle

"Hilarious and always on the mark."

—Washington Times

Key West Normal

LAURENCE SHAMES

.

DEDICATION

To Marilyn,

the mate that fate had me created for

PROLOGUE

S ome folks say you can't make this stuff up.

Who knows? Maybe they're right. I wouldn't know. I've never tried to make stuff up. I've never had to. Why would I? I live in Key West, Florida. Weird stuff happens every day here. Except, in Key West, it doesn't necessarily count as weird. After a while it just starts seeming normal. Maybe it's not what you would call average normal or most-places normal. I guess you could just say it's Key West normal.

Maybe I see more weird stuff than the typical person or even the typical Key Wester because of where I live. I don't live in a house or a bungalow or an apartment or a condo. I live in a hot dog. I don't mean a hot dog like you would eat. Where I live is in what used to be a vending wagon where a guy sold hot dogs alongside Smathers Beach, which is on the ocean side and faces south toward the Florida Straits. I should mention that Smathers is already a strange, sort of pretend-beach to begin with, because it's really made of gnarly coral nubs that the city hides under hundreds of dumptrucks full of sand at the start of every tourist season. Don't ask me where all that sand comes from. Somewhere in Florida there must be a gigantic hole in the ground that I guess gets bigger every year and will eventually cave in or maybe they'll just start calling it a lake.

Anyway, the hot dog where I live is basically a small trailer that a guy named Sonny used to hitch behind his car. Before we fixed it up to live in, it had a deep fat fryer and slosh pan for heating sauerkraut and some napkin holders and a frame for the giant containers of mustard and ketchup with those plunger tops to squirt the stuff out. You get the picture; just a basic set-up for selling franks and fries.

But what made it special is that the whole trailer was made to look like a hot dog so people would know what he was selling. The sides belly out and are painted brown like a toasted bun; the window where the guy took money and handed out the food is in the middle. The top has a big red curving wiener with a long squiggle of bright yellow mustard on it.

Usually, when the hot dog wagon was still a going operation, it would be parked halfway up the promenade, not very far from the public restrooms where I and a lot of other guys would take our showers. On one side of the hot dog wagon would be a pizza truck painted orange and green, which I guess are the colors of the Italian flag. Anyway, it made it look Italian. On the other side would be a taco truck with a sombrero on top. Then there were sno-cones and ice cream. If you happened to have some money, you could have a four-course lunch without ever putting shoes on or moving more than thirty feet from the Atlantic Ocean. I guess the trucks did a nice business during season. Tourists would line up all the way back to the seawall, and with all the different kinds of sunburn stuff they wore, you could hardly smell the sauerkraut or the pizza or the onions. Sometimes people would turn around from the cash register and give me their spare change. I never asked for it and I tried never to look at someone else's food, which I think is pretty rude. But I guess I looked hungry. Most people are really pretty nice, and besides, who has a change pocket in a bathing suit?

Anyway, at some point the hot dog guy skipped town, and that's really where this story starts. But don't ask me exactly how long ago it happened, because I'm not very good at remembering time stuff, and neither is anybody else who's lived in Key West for a lot of years. I guess it's the heat, the humidity, the being pretty much cut off from the rest of the world and what happens in it. Calendars just don't tell you much down here. Anyway, the guy skipped town and no one knew why. The rumor, which turned out not to be the real reason anyway, was that he'd never believed in things like permits or inspections or sales tax, and eventually the fines built up to where they were more than the hot dog wagon was worth. So the thing sat empty for weeks or maybe even months, who remembers? Anyway, quite a while. Stickers, like different kinds of parking tickets, I guess, started sprouting all over it. Some of the stickers were yellow, some were blue, some were red, some were pink. One evening Fred and I got to talking about it.

You'll hear more about Fred as we go along. He's my best friend and roommate, though at the time we didn't have what you'd really call a room, only a few tarps spread out in a clearing in the mangroves just east of the airport. So one evening we're sitting around our little campfire, and I ask Fred a question. This happens a lot, because I get curious about stuff that I just can't figure out. So I ask Fred. Fred's a lot smarter than I am. He has a lot more experience of the world. He understands things, how stuff works. So I say to him, just sort of thinking out loud, "I wonder what's with all the different colors."

"All *what* colors, Piney?" he says. I should mention that Piney is what he calls me, though my actual name, or at least what everyone else calls me, is Pineapple. Just Pineapple. That's it. Used to be, a very long time ago, I had a more regular name, two names actually, first and last, but the first name never suited me and I never even knew the guy that the last name came from, so I just sort of let it go. No big loss. A relief, to tell the truth. If someone shouted out that old name while I was walking down the beach, I don't think I'd even turn my head.

Anyway, I have this habit, a bad habit I guess, of sometimes just starting a conversation in the middle, picking up from stuff I've been thinking but haven't yet said aloud, so of course the other person has no idea what I'm talking about. So Fred says, "What colors, Piney?"

"The stickers," I say. "On the hot dog. There's all these different kinds."

"Different kinds of cops," Fred says. Like I told you, he knows the world, how things work. "Permit cops. Health department cops. Tax cops. They all get different color stickers."

"The pink's my favorite."

"Wagon's gonna get hauled away at some point," he says. "Has to happen. Mark my words. Prob'ly the only reason it hasn't happened yet is that the different cops can't decide whose job it is. *You take it. No, YOU take it. Not my jurisdiction. Sure ain't mine.* Passin' the buck. That's what they do. All of 'em. Lazy slobs. Sittin' in their air-conditioned cars drinkin' coffee. That's what they do. Drink coffee, act tough, then pass the buck."

Well, I knew by then that Fred sometimes got a little worked up or bitter-sounding when talking about cops or the authorities in general, and I was a little sorry I even raised the subject, though I was just curious about the stickers. Still, I didn't want to get him all upset, especially while we were eating. I should mention that Fred works way more often than I do. Day labor for cash. Roofing, demolition, cutting coconuts before they fall on cars, that type of thing. So he buys most of our food. He's very generous about it, which I appreciate, especially because, since I gave up drinking, which is another story altogether, I seem to be hungry all time. Anyway, if I remember right, that night I had ravioli and he had Beef-a-Roni. I saw he was upset about the whole business with the stickers and the different cops, so I let the subject drop.

Fred didn't. A few minutes later, he kicks a piece of driftwood to get some sparks going in the fire and scatter the mosquitoes, and he says, "Maybe we should take it."

"Take what?"

"The wagon. The hot dog."

"Take it? Um, it doesn't belong to us."

He's finished his food by then and is picking his teeth. "Don't belong to no one else neither."

Me, I'm a slow eater, a one-ravioli-at-a-time kind of person. Eat one, think about it; eat one, think about it. So I'm still working on mine. I swallow and say, "It belongs to Sonny, right? The hot dog guy."

"Used to. Not no more. It's abandoned. It's a wreck. It's anybody's. Law of the sea."

"But it isn't in the sea," I point out. "It's on land. Right next to the curb." It isn't often that I feel like I'm a step ahead of Fred, but at that moment I thought I was.

I should have known better. Without missing a beat, he says, "Yeah, but did you notice the license plate?"

"What license plate?"

"No license plate. It's gone."

That Fred sure notices a lot of things. Me, I'd mainly just been looking at the different colored stickers.

"Gone," he says again. "And no license plate means no owner. Abandoned. Ditched. Which means that one of these days, maybe even tomorrow, who knows, when the cops get their thumbs out of their fat, lazy asses long enough to figure out whose job it is, someone's gonna haul it away and stick it in an impound yard where it'll rot or eventually get crushed in the compactor and squashed down like a burger, which I guess would be almost funny, the hot dog flattened out like a burger, but it would be a big, stupid waste and not do anybody any good. Which would be a damn shame. Typical."

"Typical of what?" I say.

I guess Fred regards this as a dumb question, since he doesn't bother answering, just kicks the fire again, which makes the frogs and crickets go quiet for a few seconds. You might be noticing by now that Fred gets worked up pretty easily. Something bothers him, he starts talking about it, which you might think gets it off his chest, except kind of the opposite happens. He gets some momentum going and talks himself into being even more bothered and red-faced than he was at the start. It must be tiring to be like that. Me, I'm pretty much the opposite. I like to be calm. In fact, I'd rather be calm than just about anything else. So I just sit still for a minute or two.

Then Fred says again, "I think maybe we should take the thing. Roll it up here and live in it."

"Roll it up here?"

"It's got wheels, don't it?"

"Well, yeah, it does, but—"

"Wheels and a hitch. So we get some rope, loop it around our waist, kind of a simple harness like—"

"Like donkeys?"

"Like Clydesdales," he says. Fred's kind of a short guy, stocky, a little bow-legged, but he thinks big.

So I'm trying to picture it: The two of us yoked in, leaning way forward, sweating, grunting, pulling a giant hot dog covered with violation stickers up the A1A. Now, the sweating and the grunting, I'm okay with that part. It doesn't bother me at all. But I admit I am really scared about maybe getting caught and getting in bad trouble. "I don't know about this, Fred," I say. "We'd have to go right past a couple of motels, past the airport, there'd be cars going by, maybe even a cop car."

Fred's way ahead of me, of course. "We do it four a.m.," he says. "Road's empty. Airport's dead. Any cops on duty, they're prob'ly down on Duval breakin' up fights at closing time. Worse comes to worst, we drop the rope, sit down on the curb, and act like we don't know nothing and weren't doing anything. Play dumb. Just play dumb. Usually the best approach."

"Makes me nervous."

"Me too a little. Okay, I admit it. But havin' a place to live, Piney. Dry when it rains. Warm when it's cold. I say it's worth takin' a chance. It's not a risk-free world out there."

I know he's right but I wish he wasn't. I'm just such a wimp when it comes to trouble. Feels like I spend a lot of my life trying to avoid it. You might be thinking there's nothing special about that, everybody tries to keep out of trouble. But that doesn't go with things I've seen down here. I've seen guys who go out of their way to get in trouble, like they're always on the hunt for rules they can get caught breaking. Even dumb little rules. Like with the public shower. Sign says No Shampoo. So they bring shampoo, usually one of those little packets that motels give out and sometimes end up in the garbage. Guard calls them on it, they get nasty. Next thing you know, it's gone from shampoo or no shampoo to getting cuffs slapped on and your head pushed down while getting shoved into the squad car. Some guys seem to like that. Gives them something they need, I guess. Everybody's different.

Anyway, all I'm saying is I don't look for trouble. Mostly I just try to go unnoticed. Problem is, it's hard go unnoticed when you've got a harness on and you're towing away someone else's hot dog wagon in the middle of the night. But Fred talks me into it, of course. That's how it usually goes with us. Fred decides. I go along.

So Fred decides we should take the wagon on a night when there isn't any moon. To be honest, I don't see where this matters much, since there are orange streetlamps ten times brighter than the moon like every fifty feet along the road. But okay, it's Fred's plan. Fred gets some rope. He probably steals it from a job site, but I don't need to know that kind of thing.

So, ahead of time, we try to flatten out the path that leads to our clearing and also make it wide enough for the hot dog to pass through. This takes a lot of work with a machete. Fred has one, of course, and don't ask me where it came from. He keeps it right next to his bedroll when he's sleeping. Sometimes in the middle of the night he gives a whimper like a little baby and I can see his fingers sort of twitch toward the handle of it. I figure he's dreaming about being attacked or something, so I whisper, *it's okay, Fred* and he settles right back down again. Anyway, we had to dig out a few coral rocks and trim a few of those mangrove roots that look like teepees and are really a bear to cut with a rusty machete. But we managed. We didn't need or want much extra clearance, just enough to lug the hot dog through and then have it pretty much disappear.

So the big night finally comes. We eat early, give ourselves plenty of time to rest up. Around midnight, the planes finally stop taking off and landing. I should mention that, where we are, the planes go by so low that you can count the rivets on their wings. You can see the treads on their tires when they're landing. It's very loud, but then again, if we weren't smack dab in the middle of the approach path, there'd be a hotel or condo here and we wouldn't have a place to live. You have to take the bad with the good. Or the good with the bad. I never remember which way it goes. Anyway, it's something Fred says, and I agree.

Judging by the stars, it's around 3:30 when we head out. It's low tide, so there's a little bit of that rotten egg smell in the air. Not a strong smell, just a whiff of something extra added to the salt and dried-out seashells. It's kind of funky but I like it or maybe I'm just used to it. When we're not right under a streetlamp we can see some stars, sort of smudgy from the haze. A couple of times we see people in the mangroves by the seawall. There's a guy asleep under a turned-over rowboat. There's a guy fishing, not catching anything, but that's usually how it goes. So we're walking along, not fast, because the truth is we're both scared, and then I start to think about something and at some point I say to Fred, "What if we don't like it?"

"Don't like what, Piney?"

"The hot dog. Living in it. Sleeping inside. What if we don't like it? Would we put it back?"

"Put it back? And take a whole 'nother chance at getting caught? Plus, then it would be worse, 'cause we'd have to explain how we got it in the first place, and how long we had it, and what we used it for, and all that stuff."

I hadn't thought of the explaining part. Having to explain would make me very nervous and I'd probably get all tongue-tied and make things worse than they already were.

"If we don't like it," Fred goes on, "we drag it off to the side or push it onto the salt flat and go back to living like we are. Nothing lost."

"But then it would go to waste," I say.

"Yeah, what of it?"

"You said you'd hate to see it go to waste."

"Piney, it's not a perfect world. Things go to waste sometimes."

"So why's it different if we waste it or someone else does?"

He gives me a certain look he gets when I'm asking too many questions. "Why are you making this so complicated? You looking to bail? You chickening out on me?"

I guess I should mention that Fred has had six or eight beers since dinner, so he's probably feeling braver than I am. I remember that feeling—drinking to keep up my nerve, I mean. Usually turned out not to be a great idea. Then again, I've never really understood what's so terrible about chickening out. Guys make it sound like it's the worst thing you can do, like you'll never live it down. I just don't get that. Say guys are diving headfirst into water where they can't see the bottom. At the last second, you chicken out. This is something to be ashamed of? Like I say, I don't get it. Anyway, to me this was not a question of chickening out or not chickening out, but a question that I gave Fred my word that I'd go through with this, so I told him again I would.

So we keep walking down the promenade. Every now and then a scooter goes by, every now and then a car. I feel a stab in my stomach every time. Finally we reach the hot dog. It looks awfully big to drag around but awfully small to live in. We sit down on the seawall to rest and try to look innocent. Then Fred moseys over and casually looks at how the hitch is set up. Then he backs off like he's really not that interested. Then he bends down like maybe he dropped a dime or something and ties the rope around the hitch. Then he looks back at me, so I guess there's no getting out of it now. My mouth is dry. It's hard to breathe. I push myself up from the seawall and sort of lasso myself inside the loop of the rope next to Fred.

He tightens down his face and says, "Okay. Ready? One...two...three!"

We pull. Nothing happens. The rope sort of squeezes us together and neither of us has a good angle. The hot dog doesn't budge. To be honest, I'm relieved. I'm thinking, okay, we tried, we kept our word to each other, now let's go back and sleep on the ground. But Fred doesn't give up easy. He steps out of the harness and walks around the wagon. "Tires are out of round," he says. "Happens sometimes when a trailer sits too long. They'll come back into shape once we get it moving. Come on, one big pull."

So we bear down and grunt and strain and, sure enough, it turns out Fred is right about the tires. They squeak a little then make a ca-chunk sound when we horse them past the flat part and then they start to roll. Once the hot dog's moving on the pavement, it's really not that tough to pull.

Except at some point it starts to feel like there's a weight moving around inside the wagon, rocking it a little bit, sometimes left, sometimes right, sometimes forward, sometimes back.

I ask Fred if he feels it. "Prob'ly something busted loose," he says. "Maybe the tub that held the French fry grease, something like that."

We're halfway to the airport when we hear a car coming up fast behind us. I'm trying to hold my bowels together but the car just cruises past. Red convertible. Tourist probably. Maybe didn't even notice us. Maybe just thought it was normal for down here, two guys dragging a hot dog by a rope.

Up at the east end of the island, the road makes a big left turn, so when we reach the curve we know we're almost home. But that's also the hardest part, because now we have to leave the pavement and go cross-country over rocks and potholes and clumps of weeds with spines and thorns. My feet are hurting and the hot dog is bouncing and leaning and things are clattering inside. We get to the path that leads into our clearing, but of course it turns out that we didn't hack it out quite wide enough, so mangrove branches are scraping and slapping against the sides and now and then one of the tires needs to be jackassed over a root, and whatever it is that's loose inside is rolling around like a pinball and keeps changing the momentum. So the last fifty feet or so are really a bear.

We're sweating bullets but we get it done. With a few extra heaves we get the thing positioned at a nice angle near our burned-out campfire and then we finally get to drop the rope. I don't mind telling you my hands are pretty raw by then. I guess Fred's are too, since he spits on his palms then rubs them together. Then he walks around the hot dog, sizing it up all different ways, with this look on his face like he just bought himself a brand new Cadillac. I follow him around and I have to say I feel pretty good too about the whole set-up. The hot dog looks...well, I don't know exactly how to say this...looks like it belongs there, like it's been there all along, even though, two minutes before, it wasn't.

Anyway, Fred goes over to his cooler and grabs a beer. It's just about dawn by now, still dark, but at that point where the sky is just starting to be a different color than the leaves and branches. He says, "Well, we did it, Piney. I always knew we could. Never doubted it for a second."

I don't believe he really means this, but that's Fred.

"Our new home," he goes on. "We'll fix it up nice. So let's

have a look. Go ahead, Piney, do the honors, open 'er up."

He nods toward the low little door at the back of the wagon. I walk over to it, but touching the handle worries me. I mean, it bothered me a little to lug the whole hot dog away, but the thought of going inside it scares me more. I guess when you're used to living outside, the inside of places makes you nervous. But I take a deep breath and pull on the handle. The door doesn't open.

"It's stuck," I say.

"Pull harder," says Fred.

So I pull harder. Same deal. "Guess it's locked," I say.

"Couldn't be much of a lock on a dinky door like that. Just give it a good yank."

"What if I break it?"

"If it breaks, it breaks. Gotta get in sometime."

He has a point there, so I take another breath, prop one foot against the fender, brace my wrist with my free hand, and yank for all I'm worth. I get this funny feeling that something's yanking back, but after a little tug of war it finally lets go and I hear a grunt and a groan and then the door flies open and I see a man in blue pajamas and brown slippers perched off-balance on the ledge of the doorway, still trying to hang on to the inside latch as the door is swinging open. He teeters for half a second then takes a flying header out of the hot dog, does a cramped-up half-somersault in mid-air, ends up making a face-plant on a slab of coral rock, then lies there on the ground with his arms and legs splayed out, still as a crushed bug.

For a couple seconds I just stand there. I guess I'm in shock. I have no idea what to say or do. Finally I just yell out, "Hey, I'm sorry!"

He doesn't answer. He doesn't move.

"Hey, I didn't mean to hurt you," I yell again.

Still nothing. So I go over to him, squat down low, give

him a little push on the shoulder. By now I'm thinking, Oh my God, he's dead. And it's my fault. Maybe I gave him a heart attack and he was dead before he even hit the ground. Or maybe he just crushed his skull. Either way, it's on me. I killed him. I didn't mean to, but it doesn't matter what you mean, it matters what happens. I'm starting to cry. I feel so bad and guilty that I'd gladly change places with the dead guy on the ground. At least then I wouldn't have to worry about hurting anyone or getting into trouble anymore.

Anyway, I'm thinking all this, and meanwhile Fred comes over and is also looking at the dead guy, but he has a whole different way of dealing with the situation. Like I said, he's way smarter than me and way more practical. He gives the guy a little nudge with his foot. Not a kick, just a test nudge. Nothing happens. Finally, he says, "Piney, maybe this whole thing wasn't such a hot idea."

"Maybe not," I say, looking at the guy stretched out on the ground.

"But what's done is done," he says.

"Yeah, I guess it is."

"And if we get caught with a dead guy here, we're really fucked."

"Yeah, I guess we are."

"So let's get moving, Piney. Before it gets any lighter. You want the arms or the legs?"

1

Except, as it turned out, the man in blue pajamas who'd come flying out of the hot dog, and whose name was Peter Kaplan, was not dead but only briefly knocked unconscious, and when Fred and Pineapple started to lift what they thought was his corpse, he surprised them by kicking out a foot and twitching back a hand. So they dropped him again. He groaned, rolled around a moment, and finally sat up. The sun had just peeked over the horizon and a low wet glare was slicing through the mangroves. He squinted around the clearing, then at Pineapple and Fred, and said, "Where the hell am I?"

Fred didn't want too many other people to know about his and Piney's special spot, so by instinct he played it cagey. "Not far from where you started."

Kaplan blinked and looked around some more. He was a compact fellow, within a few years either way of fifty, very early-retired as an English professor at one of New York's less prestigious colleges. He had a brainy-looking but rather nervous face—a bit twitchy at the corners of the mouth and the edges of the eyes—and curly brown hair that was receding on top and showing just a hint of grey at the temples. He wasn't bleeding but he had a raw red bump on his forehead.

Pineapple, still sniffling a bit, said, "Jeez, I'm so glad you're okay. I was really scared I killed you. But look, we didn't know someone else was already living in the hot dog. We thought it was up for grabs. But fair is fair. If you have first dibs on it, it's yours."

Kaplan said, "What?"

"The hot dog," Fred put in. "Guess it's yours as much as

ours. If you're living in it, that's cool. We'll put it back. No hard feelings. I'm Fred, by the way. This is Pineapple."

Kaplan gingerly ran fingertips over the bump on his head as if trying to decide if he was really awake. "Fred. Pineapple. Okay, fine. I'm Peter. Nice to meet you. But listen, I have no idea what you're talking about."

"The hot dog," Pineapple tried to explain. "We're just saying if you're already living in it—"

"Living in it? You think I'm living in the hot dog? I don't live in a hot dog. I live in a house."

Fred said, "So why were you in the hot dog at four in the morning?"

"In your pajamas," added Piney.

Kaplan looked down at his lap. He seemed for the moment to have forgotten he was in his pj's. "Okay, I guess it looks a little odd," he admitted. "But the reason I was there...well, it's really pretty simple. I was looking for my cat."

"Your cat?" said Pineapple.

"My cat. Sasha. I really love my cat. More than anything. Except my wife, I mean. She sometimes wanders off at night."

"Your wife wanders off?" said Fred.

"Not my wife. The cat. The cat wanders off. Sometimes she used to wander off to the hot dog wagon. Back when it was still in business, I mean. For some odd reason she really liked the guy who ran it."

"Oh, I remember him," said Piney. "Sonny. Big heavy-set guy in a dirty apron with the strings hanging down. Sort of a tough guy, but nice. Gave me a frank now and then if he had an extra at the end of the day. Kind of overcooked and wrinkly. Nice of him, though."

"Well, he once gave my cat a French fry with ketchup on it. Which I happen to think is a very wrong thing to do. You don't give scraps to other people's pets. It's dangerous. Food allergies. What if they're on a special diet? High fiber, low fiber, whatever. But Sasha loved the French fry and after that she loved Sonny. Which, to be honest, sort of hurt my feelings, especially since at home she's such a finicky eater, only a certain kind of cat food and, even then, only if she's in a certain kind of mood. Sometimes I worry she's starving. My wife's tried everything. She's Burmese."

Fred said, "Your wife's Burmese?"

"Not my wife. The cat. The cat's Burmese. Will you please let it go about my wife?"

The sun had gotten higher. The air was drying out and the shadows of the mangrove roots and leaves took on sharper edges. A whirring noise started up as the morning's first outbound flight began to taxi on the nearby runway. A whiff of jet fuel mingled with the smells of sea and salt flat.

Fred said, "Okay, got it, it's the cat that's Burmese. Sorry, I'm a little tired. And I've had some beers. Want one?"

"Thanks, no. Little early for me."

"Suit yourself. But what I'm still trying to picture is why you were actually *in* the hot dog."

"Look, the cat usually sleeps at my feet. Right between them. Makes a little valley in the bed. At some point I sense she isn't there. I call her. Nothing. I go to the kitchen. I go out to the yard. No cat. Now I'm getting worried. So I get in the car and drive to the promenade—"

"In your pajamas," Pineapple put in.

"Right. In my pajamas. Look, it's Key West. It's the middle of the night. I don't plan on running into anyone I know. It's not like I'm going to the Oscars. Who cares I'm in my pajamas? And another thing. I take sleeping pills. Can't stop my mind running round and round without them. My head hits the pillow, my brain wakes up instead of getting sleepy. So I take pills. So if I wake up in the middle of the night, I'm a little groggy. Probably not thinking my very best.

So I drive to the ocean, park the car, and start looking for the cat. Then I think I hear her meow. I'm not sure I hear it. It's pretty faint. And it's human nature, you're looking for something, you want to imagine that you're finding it, right? So maybe I hear her, and maybe the sound is from the hot dog truck, plus maybe I'm a little foggy from the Ambien, so I try the door, and it opens after a little fiddling, and I go in, and that's when you guys come along."

"So the cat was inside?" asked Piney.

"No. She wasn't."

Fred said, "So why'd you stay in the hot dog? Once it started moving, I mean?"

Kaplan looked down at the remains of Fred's and Piney's campfire. His right eye twitched at the outside corner. "Well, I guess I panicked. Didn't know what was going on. Sort of froze. I do that sometimes. Panic, I mean. I have pills for that too, but I didn't have them with me. I mean, I didn't plan on getting kidnapped."

"You're not kidnapped," said Piney reassuringly. "We're just looking for a place to live."

Kaplan glanced up at the vending wagon he'd been yanked out of and tried for a moment to imagine it as a home. True, it was dilapidated and cramped, but the yellow mustard on top of the brick-red frankfurter gave it a certain cheerfulness. It might actually be sort of cozy.

Fred said, "So you won't tell on us, will you? About taking the hot dog, I mean."

Kaplan shrugged. "No. Why would I?"

Pineapple said, "That's nice of you. I hope you find your cat."

"Thanks. I'd be pretty crushed if I lost her."

He choked up as he said this, which really got to Pineapple. He himself had never had a pet. Dogs always belonged to other people and generally were unwelcoming to him. The stray cats all over Key West sometimes seemed like kindred spirits but he'd never tried to make friends with any. After a moment, he heard himself say, "I'd really like to help you find her."

Kaplan said, "Well, that's awfully nice of you, but—"

"No, really. After all the stuff we've put you through. Made you panic. Knocked you out cold. Please, I'd like to help. Come on, let's start looking."

2

S o the two of them left the clearing, rounded the curve
next to the airport, and started walking down the
promenade. It was nearly eight a.m. by then. The sun
had gone from yellow to white and the morning breeze was
raising pointy little wavelets on the water. People were out
jogging and skating and biking, or sitting on the seawall and
drinking coffee. No one seemed terribly surprised to see a
smallish man in blue pajamas and brown slippers and with a
big bump on his head walking with a rangy, ragged fellow
who looked less tropical than Appalachian. This was Key
West. People wore what they felt like wearing and walked
with anyone they felt like walking with.

But they didn't find the cat.

They walked past the row of vending wagons, still
shuttered at that hour of the day; the absent hot dog, like a
missing tooth, made the spacing of the others seem awkward
and off-balance. They continued on to the public restrooms
and showers where some guys brought shampoo and got in
trouble. A couple of times they saw stray cats skulking by,
but nothing resembling a groomed and beloved Burmese.
Finally they reached the place where Kaplan had left his car.
"Well, Pineapple," he said, "I guess that's about as much as
we can do for now."

"I'll keep looking. Don't worry. She'll turn up."

"Hope so. Thanks. She has a tag on her collar. You'll call
me if you find her?"

"Um, I don't have a phone."

"Ah. Well, there's also an address."

"So it would be okay if I came to your house?"

"Sure, if you have the cat...No wait, that didn't come out right. I mean, sure you can come to the house. Anytime. Twenty-three Poorhouse Lane. Down past the cemetery."

"Okay, thanks. And you're always welcome at the hot dog."

They shook hands. Kaplan got into his car, hung a U-turn, and threaded his way through the narrow streets of Old Town and around the above-ground graveyard to his house. It was not a fancy house but that morning it seemed a palace—two stories, blue shutters on the windows, a front yard with bougainvillea and hibiscus shrubs, a porch with some gingerbread fringe and a couple of rocking chairs.

His wife, Meg, was sitting in one of them next to a small wicker table, wearing a light cotton robe, drinking coffee and eating a bran muffin. She sprang up as soon as her husband pulled into the driveway. "Peter!" she called out. "Where've you been? I've been worried sick."

This in itself was very unusual. Meg Kaplan was not a worrier. She generally left the worrying to Peter, since it came so naturally to him and he seemed, in a way, to enjoy it. She herself was serene. She did yoga. She believed things turned out as they were meant to. She was the same age as Peter, a former teaching colleague, though from the Eastern Philosophy department, so her face was unlined, her brow unfurrowed, and her wide-spaced green eyes steady and calm. She was fit and lean and did Pilates and could put her palms flat on the floor.

Her husband called back from the driveway, "I've been looking for the cat."

"She's home," Meg said serenely. "In the house. Asleep."

"Oh, thank God."

He climbed the two steps to the porch. They had a brief hug. Seeing him close up, she said, "What happened to your head?"

"Long story. But the cat's okay? Not hurt or anything? When did she come home?"

"Not long after you left. That bruise looks nasty, Peter. Let me put some arnica on it. Or maybe ginger root."

"Let's please not start with the herbal healing bullshit, okay? It just wants to be left alone. So you're sure she's okay?"

"She's fine. I called the police."

"About the cat?"

"Not about the cat. About you. I reported you missing. They said they'd look."

He let out a sharp, quick laugh that made his head hurt. "That's a good one. Like the Key West cops ever find a missing person? They can't find their patrol car half the time. Any more coffee? Another muffin, maybe?"

She went into the house and came out a moment later with a mug, a muffin, and the arnica cream. He let her put some on the bump. That's often how it went with them. She'd make a suggestion, he'd pooh-pooh it, then accept with gratitude. He lightly held her waist while she dabbed the bruise.

"So how'd it happen?" she asked.

Between sips of coffee and nibbles of muffin, he told her the story. The hot dog wagon; his panic; getting pulled up past the airport then yanked down onto a rock; what nice guys Pineapple and Fred turned out to be.

She said, "So this was the hot dog wagon that Sonny used to run?"

"Only hot dog wagon up there."

"Well, small world. I have a story for you, too."

"Uh-oh."

"Why *uh-oh*? Why assume it's an *uh-oh* story? Maybe it's a happy story. Why's *uh-oh* your first reaction?"

"I don't know. Experience?"

She picked up some muffin crumbs with the flat of her thumb and daintily brought them to her lips. "Well, anyway, the story is that it was Sonny from the hot dog wagon who brought Sasha home."

"That guy? He hasn't been around for months."

"Correct. And now he's back. Can I have a little of your coffee? Mine got cold."

He handed her his mug.

She took a sip, passed it back, and casually went on. "And right now he's sleeping in our guest room."

A little coffee sloshed onto Peter's pajama leg. "What?"

"It was kind of strange. I mean, it was the middle of the night. He shows up with the cat, says he found her wandering up along the promenade near the hot dog wagon. He remembered her, of course, so he read her tag and brought her home. I thanked him, we chatted for a few minutes, and he left. Maybe half an hour later, maybe even less, he came back. The second time he didn't look so good. Seemed really upset. I asked him what was wrong. He didn't seem to want to go into it. But he seemed stressed out and exhausted and like he had no place to go. And he was so nice about the cat. I mean, he didn't have to bring her home. So I invited him to stay here."

"Invited him to stay? Just like that? A stranger off the street?"

"Not a total stranger. Besides, Sasha likes him. She's in there with him now."

"In the guest bedroom with him? He's sleeping with my cat?"

"You can't tell a cat who to sleep with, Peter."

He drummed his fingers on the little table, pushed aside the rest of his muffin. "Why not? You can have the decency to close the door if you're a guest. Or *someone* should've closed the door. Anyway, it's very disappointing. I thought she was classier than that. Rare, fancy, Burmese. Ha! One stinking French fry. One stinking squirt of ketchup and now she's in the sack with him like some tart picked up in an alley. It just seems so cheap." He brooded for a moment, the bruise on his forehead turning redder, then pushed himself up by the arms of his chair. "Well, I'm going in there. I'm going to wake him up. Wake him up and tell him it's checkout time. Right this second."

Meg said softly, "You'll do nothing of the kind. It would be awfully rude. And for no reason. Let the poor guy sleep."

"With my cat?" he protested, but he lowered himself into the chair again.

His wife stroked the back of his hand with her fingertips. "Honey, you're a little overwrought. You're dealing with a lot of cortisol right now—"

"Cortisol, my eye. Let's please not start with the holistic bullshit—"

"And I really think this will all be fine if you just sleep a couple hours."

"Sleep? How can I sleep when this bun-stuffing, sauerkraut-slinging lout is shacked up with my cat?"

"Look, he'll probably be gone by the time you wake up. And Sasha will be back in bed with you."

"I'm not so sure I'll let her in. The little slut."

"Why don't you decide that later, when you're rested? How about a back rub and some melatonin?"

3

It was early afternoon when Peter woke up. His head hurt less. The house was quiet. The sun was shining.

But Sonny wasn't gone.

In fact he was sitting in a lounge chair next to the Kaplans' backyard dipping pool, munching a sandwich that appeared to be avocado and sprouts on Meg's homemade whole-wheat toast. For a long moment Peter just spied on him through a chink in the Venetian blind in the master bedroom. The visitor's black hair was wet from a swim. He was wearing aviator shades that perched a bit uneasily on his broad squashed nose. He didn't have a shirt on. He was broad and bulky, with massive arms and a ropy neck, but he wasn't fat; maybe it was just the greasy apron in the hot dog truck that had made him look that way before.

Sasha was curled up at his feet. He squeezed a squib of avocado out of the sandwich and fed it to the cat straight off his finger. This struck Peter as very unhygienic. Plus he felt undignified and ridiculous spying through a Venetian blind on someone in his own backyard. Why was he reduced to this? Why did his wife have to be so goddamn nice to everyone? Clearly, it would fall to him to be the heavy. He resolved to go outside and tell their guest in a firm but civil way that it was time for him to finish his sandwich and scram.

He got out of bed, washed his face, and pulled on a pair of shorts. On his way to the backyard, he saw a note from Meg on the kitchen counter. It said she was going out for extra groceries. Sonny would be staying for dinner.

He pulled down on the dark worry-sacs beneath his eyes

and went out through the sliding door to the pool. The palm fronds were rustling softly. The air had taken on the baked smell of high afternoon. The cat pretty much ignored him. He made a point of ignoring her in return. He said, "Hello, Sonny."

The man in the lounge chair placed what was left of his sandwich on a table at his elbow and answered before he'd finished chewing. "Hey. Peter, right? I remember now. The guy who didn't like it that I fed his cat."

"I still don't like it."

Sonny let that pass and gestured enthusiastically around the property. "Nice place ya got."

"So glad you're enjoying it."

"And that Meg is one great gal. You're a lucky man, my friend."

"Yes I am. I know." He sat down on the edge of a slatted chair in the shade of a blue umbrella. "But, um, Sonny, it was nice of you to bring the cat home, and I know my wife has invited you for dinner, which is fine, great, terrific, but, um, just between ourselves, it's kind of a smallish house, and we're not really used to having company around, and I don't really find it that comfortable, and, well, I really don't understand why the hell you're still here."

"Well, yeah, it's kind of a crazy situation. I can't disagree wit' ya on that. Ya got any beer?"

The question was so abrupt yet mild as to be totally disarming. Peter said, "I think there's a few in the fridge."

Heavily but not without grace, Sonny spun out of the lounge chair. "Want one while I'm up?"

Peter was not a day-drinker and didn't particularly feel like a beer. He heard himself say, "Yeah. Sure. Why not?"

The visitor padded off to the kitchen. As soon as he had gone, Sasha slunk over to Peter to be stroked. He gave her a wounded and disapproving look but stroked her anyway.

When Sonny came back with the beers, she lifted her tail, showed Peter her butt, and returned to the foot of the lounge.

"Cheers," said the guest.

"Cheers," came the halfhearted reply. He took a sip. "So, Sonny, about this so-called crazy situation—"

"Yeah, crazy is right. Well, listen, Pete—"

"It's Peter. No one calls me Pete."

"Okay. Sorry. But here's the thing. I'd like to tell ya about it. I really would. I mean, it'd be a relief to tell somebody, maybe have somebody help me think it through. But that might not be fair. I mean, it could be dangerous."

"Dangerous?"

"I mean, ya know, you and the missus, you've been so nice to me, I wouldn't want to cause ya any trouble."

"Well, you already have. No offense."

Sonny swigged some beer and smacked his lips. "No offense back, Peter, but so far this ain't trouble. Inconvenience maybe. For which I apologize. I really do. But what I'm dealin' wit', well, it could be real trouble."

Peter wavered between caution and curiosity but managed to keep his mouth shut. He sipped some beer and looked accusingly at the cat, who was rolling on her back and showing her belly like a common whore.

"But since you asked," Sonny went on, "it's about the hot dog wagon. The craziest goddamn thing happened last night."

"Oh?"

"Yeah. I go over there, first time in like forever, the wagon is exactly where I left it months ago. It's got some tickets stuck on it, but other'n that, it looks exactly the same. So I'm just about to go inside, and then I hear the cat from over by the seawall. Now it so happens I like cats, and this cat in particular, who of course I remember 'cause she's my buddy."

"Actually, she's my buddy," Peter said.

"Whatever. So I hear the cat, and it's the middle of the night, and I look at her tag, and I see that where she lives—here, I mean—is pretty far from where I find her, so I'm concerned, so I put her in the car and drive her over, and that's when I meet your lovely wife. You with me so far?"

"Yeah. Sure. Of course."

"So here's the crazy part. I hand over the cat. Your wife and I swap a few words. I drive back to the beach, up to where the wagon was, and it's gone. How fuckin' weird is that? Months and months it sits right where it was, and then, just when I come back, it disappears. I mean, what are the fuckin' odds?"

"Steep, I guess," said Peter. He briefly hid his face behind the beer bottle but then gave in to curiosity. "So you came back to town to run the hot dog stand again?"

"Run it? No. Hell no. Look, it's complicated. And not right I drag you into the whole business. But anyway, since you asked, no, I wasn't planning to run the stand again. I don't even own the thing. But I'm in charge of it, it's my responsibility, and if it's gone, I got a big fat fuckin' problem on my hands. Which makes me pretty goddamn mad 'cause it ain't a problem I deserve. And I'll tell ya one other thing. A lotta guys, if someone handed them a problem like this and they caught the guy who did it, ya know what they might do, just as a matter of principle? They might break some knees, bash in some teeth, stomp a few ribs. I mean, there's a code about these things. Ya don't mess with someone else's stuff and make big problems for them. I mean, some guys would say that deserves at least a beating. Am I right?"

"Um, yeah, definitely. Can't have people stealing hot dog wagons."

"Damn straight." He pulled on his beer and brooded on

his loss and on the sheer mystery of the whole business. Then he said, "But hey, wait a sec. You were out lookin' for the cat too last night, right? Your wife said you were lookin' for the cat. Said that when I brought her home."

"Well, um, yeah, that's true."

"You go up to the beach at all?"

"Well, sort of up that way, yeah."

"So did you happen to notice if the hot dog was there when you were there?"

"Was the hot dog there?" mulled Peter, softly and deliberately. "Hmm, I'm trying to remember. Was it there? Did I see it? Um, no, I don't think so. I think it must've been gone already."

"Gone already. Fuckin' unbelievable. Ten, fifteen minutes. Ya know what I'm thinkin'? That sonofabitch Citarella musta had a plan. Bastard's settin' me up."

"Citarella?"

"Never mind. I shouldn't go there. But what I'm thinkin' is that someone musta come along wit' a truck and a hitch all set up and ready to go, and pulled the thing off-island."

Peter eagerly nodded his agreement. "Yeah, towed it somewhere with a truck. Off-island. That's the only way it makes sense."

Sonny finished his beer. "The bastard. And now I got this big fat fuckin' problem. Some guys would say that someone's gonna pay big time for that."

Peter smiled weakly. Then he heard the clatter of Meg's bicycle pulling up the walkway from the street. He thought it would be an excellent idea to get up and help her with the groceries.

4

"Meg, you didn't tell him, did you?" Peter whispered.

They were standing in the kitchen. She was reaching deep into the Fausto's bag and pulling out broccoli, spring mix, snapper fillets. One by one, he took the items from her hands and stashed them on neat shelves or in orderly bins in the fridge. As on a bucket brigade, there was a flow, a sway, a dance to the transfers. The two of them had been married a long time and had the rhythm down pat. "Tell him what?" she said. "And why are you whispering?"

"About Pineapple and Fred. About them having the hot dog."

"Um, no, we didn't talk about it."

"Good, because if he finds out, he'll break all their bones."

"Really? You think he's a violent person?"

"Well, who do you think he is, Mahatma Gandhi?"

"I don't know. I just don't think he has a violent aura."

"Aura, shmaura. He just got done talking to me about smashing knees and knocking out teeth and kicking ribs in."

"Okay, so he's a little macho, a little rough around the edges. Probably didn't have all the advantages that some of us—"

"And can we please not start with the advantages bullshit? The man was talking ambulances, mayhem."

"Talking isn't doing. Besides, look how much the cat likes him. Sasha wouldn't like him if she sensed he was a violent man."

"Sasha's a tramp. You should've seen her making a spectacle of herself out there. Practically like a four-legged pole dancer. Practically like she wasn't spayed. That look in her eyes. Embarrassing."

"Honey, you been drinking?"

"I had a beer. It was Sonny's idea. I don't even know why I had one. I didn't want it. I'm just all keyed up with this knee-breaker in the house and the cat ignoring me."

"I'm sorry your feelings are a little hurt. It'll pass."

"Possibly. But in the meantime, are you sure you didn't mention where the hot dog ended up? Or Pineapple and Fred?"

"Pretty sure."

"You talked this morning, right? You made him lunch. Do you remember what you talked about?"

"Nutrition."

"Nutrition?"

"I was explaining that there was just as much protein in that sandwich as a hot dog, but without the bad fat and the nitrates and the coloring. Frankly, he didn't seem that interested."

"Score one for him," said Peter. He snapped the corners of the empty grocery bag so that it folded flat and bent down low to stash it in a floor-level cupboard for recycling. While still in a squat, he said, "Oh shit."

"What? You throw your back out?"

"My back is fine," he answered, though the mere suggestion that he'd thrown it out gave him a sharp twinge on one side. "But with all this worrying about Pineapple and Fred, I just realized I'm also in line to get my teeth knocked out. I mean, I guess I'm an accomplice."

"Accomplice to what?"

"Look, I was *in* the hot dog when they rolled it away. And then, just two minutes ago, I lied to him about it. I told him it was already gone when I got there."

"Why'd you lie? Lying never changes anything. Only makes everything more complicated."

"I'm aware of that, Confucius, thank you very much. I lied because I had to. To protect those guys. Anyway, he seems to think somebody named Citarella towed the thing off-island."

"Citarella? Who's Citarella?"

"I have no idea. He mentioned the name then stopped himself. But there was murder in his voice when he said it."

Meg said, "That sounds like an exaggeration. No one could kill you with their voice."

"No? Have you tried listening to Tony Bennett lately?"

She let that pass. "Well, look," she said, "if he thinks it was towed off-island, that's good, right?"

Peter declined to be reassured. "Yeah, but how do you *get* off-island? By driving past the airport and right past their little clearing. What if he happens to look in?"

"I guess that could be a problem," she admitted. "Maybe you should warn your pals."

"They don't have a phone."

"You could drive up there. Or take a bike ride."

"What if he follows me?"

"Why would he do that?"

"I don't know. 'Cause I'm a worst-case scenario kind of guy, I guess. But look, I just lied to him and I'm a lousy liar. I mumbled. I fumbled. Maybe he saw right through me. Maybe he's suspicious now. What if I lead him straight to them?"

Meg plugged in the blender and started gathering ingredients to make herself a smoothie. "Peter, you can't go through life worrying about every bad thing that has even the tiniest chance of happening."

"Why not? It's working for me so far. But look, this whole business, stolen hot dogs, knee-breakers eating avocado sandwiches at poolside, I just don't like one single thing about it. I just don't see it ending well."

His wife calmly and unhurriedly mixed yogurt, apple cider, mango, blueberry, banana. When the ingredients had all been added but before she switched on the screaming blade, she said, "Can I make a suggestion, honey? Just to try to calm things down and maybe simplify a little? If you're so worried about the bad things that could happen with the hot dog, how about if you and your friends just put it back where it was?"

This common-sense approach was somehow stupefying to Peter. "Put it back? But then Fred and Piney wouldn't have a place to live."

"Look, I'm on their side. Of course I am. But when you have a place, you can always lose it, right? That goes for everybody. Fire, flood, hurricane. The place you live in could be gone tomorrow. The place *we* live in could be gone tomorrow. People don't like to think about it, but it's true."

She started the blender. After the whispering in the kitchen it sounded as loud as a landing airplane. She switched it off some seconds later and the roar died back to a whine on its way to silence.

Peter said, "Well, I'd just hate to see them sleeping on the ground again."

"Me too. But I don't see how they can have it both ways. Either they give up the hot dog or they take their chances with Sonny. And it really should be their decision, don't you think?"

"Well, yeah, sure, I guess. It's just that it kind of sucks either way."

Meg poured her smoothie into a tall glass and serenely appraised its silky texture and the little tumbling bits of blueberry. "Unless it all works out just wonderfully and everybody ends up happy."

Her husband looked at her with awe. "Must be amazing to be you," he said, then immediately got back to fretting. "But what if they're putting it back and Sonny happens by? He'll freak. He won't wait for an explanation. He'll start hurting people."

Meg sipped some smoothie then dabbed her lips on a napkin. "Sonny won't happen by."

"No? What makes you so sure? Because it wouldn't fit your happy ending?"

"No, because we'll know exactly where Sonny is. Sonny'll be in the guest room with the cat. Asleep."

"Oh, Christ, you've invited him to stay again?"

"Not yet. But I think we should. It's the safest way, right? Send him off to bed, we know he won't be wandering around, then you go tell your friends and they can make up their minds."

"So I'll be up all freakin' night again?"

"You don't sleep much anyway, honey."

"No, but I'm in bed, at least. I have my eyeshade, my pillow."

"We'll have dinner on the early side. Maybe he'll be tired."

"How about me? I'm fuckin' exhausted."

"Have some smoothie. Very energizing. Very restorative."

"Restorative. You know what I would find restorative? Not some yogurt and a smushed banana. What I would find restorative would be having my house back and having my cat back. So please let's have an early night and get this over with."

5

But they didn't have an early night.

Sonny, it turned out, was a slow eater. Slow but relentless. He had two servings of snapper and two bowls of quinoa, gruffly but graciously handing out compliments and thanks for every course. When the wine was gone, he asked with his usual directness and utter lack of qualm if there happened to be another bottle handy. For dessert he had two slices of Key lime pie and asked Meg if it would be too much trouble to make some coffee. Then, finally, while Peter was fiercely hoping that their guest would take his full belly up the stairs and into bed, he blithely announced that he'd be heading out for a nightcap with a friend—where on the island he didn't say—but promised to be quiet as a mouse when he returned.

Peter didn't dare to run his errand while Sonny was at large, so he loaded the dishwasher and tried to stay mad at the cat. This whole crazy business was all her fault. If she hadn't gone wandering off, none of it would have happened. Plus now she seemed to be gaga for their freeloading lout of a guest. He gave her a chiding glance as she vamped around the kitchen. The look she flashed back at him was not exactly innocent, just immune from any sort of criticism whatsoever. With a single bound, she leaped up onto the counter, right next to the sink, and waited for Peter to turn the water on to a perfect trickle so she could drink straight from the faucet. He did as she demanded.

"So this Citarella," Sonny was saying. "Frankie Citarella. He's always had it in for me. For years now. But sneaky, like. Like we're pals except we ain't. Didn't start that way. Started off we were pretty chummy. Then somethin' changed, and it's like he's out to screw me. Been that way pretty much as long as I can remember now."

He and his friend and his friend's chihuahua were sitting at a high-top on the porch at Ducky's, an outdoor bar on the quiet end of Duval Street, or what had been the quiet end when Duval Street had a quiet end. Now the cafes and tequila joints and piercing parlors and CBD shops stretched pretty much from the harbor to the ocean. Neon-lighted pedi-cabs and hookers of innumerable shades of gender cruised along for business at every hour of the day or night. Occasionally someone went by on a unicycle or a skateboard naked except for possibly a bit of body paint. Why not? It was normal for Key West. The weather was mild and no one seemed to mind.

"So, what changed?" asked the friend, whose name was Bert d'Ambrosia, widely known as Bert the Shirt in honor of his extensive and flamboyant wardrobe. He was a very old man, though no one knew exactly how old, and it would have accomplished nothing to put a number on his age. How old was a rock? How old was the sky? In Key West it just seemed like Bert had always been there. Decades were like minutes to him. He stepped across generations like they were shrinking puddles on a hot sidewalk. He knew everyone. He talked to everyone. He was tall and lean, a bit shrunken in the chest and shoulders, but not to the point where you couldn't tell what a formidable figure he'd been. He still had a full head of silver hair that was tinged the yellow-bronze of old newspaper at the ends. He had a big banana nose; black, deep-set, no-bullshit eyes; long-lobed ears; a thick-lipped and facetious mouth; and was dressed that evening in a shirt of lavender silk with navy-blue piping and a monogram in flowing script on the left chest pocket.

"What changed?" said Sonny. "Well, I'm really not sure. But I kinda got an inkling."

"Yeah? So what's the inkling?"

"Just between ourselves?"

"No, I'm gonna scream it from the rooftops. Course it's between ourselves."

Sonny sighed. It was a surprisingly soft and wistful sound to be coming from so large a frame. "Well, I used to, ya know, have a thing with his wife."

"A thing?"

"Yeah, ya know, a thing."

"Like, a sexual thing?"

"Well, yeah. Partly."

"Like, you were pokin' 'er?"

"That's not exactly how I'd put it, but okay, yeah."

The old man slowly and sorrowfully shook his head. "Sorry, Sonny, but that ain't right and you know it ain't right. I mean, you know the rules as good as anyone. Pokin' someone's wife. You're lucky ya still got testicles."

"But wait, hang on a second, Bert. Ya got me wrong. It's not like she was his wife at the time."

"Excuse me?"

"This thing we had, it was a long time ago. Back in Brooklyn. Before Citarella even knew her."

"Ah. So you weren't pokin' his wife."

"No."

"So why'dya say ya were?"

"I didn't say that. You said that. Anyway, she was my girlfriend at the time. And it wasn't just a pokin' thing. Very far from it. Truth is, I was crazy about her. Cecile, her name is. She's beautiful. Gorgeous. And she just has something. I don't know what it is. Her smile, her laugh, who knows? Just something. Anyway, she ended up dumping me. For him. Why? I still don't know, ya want the truth. Maybe she figured he was goin' places and I was goin' nowhere. Hard to blame 'er if she thought that. But here's the part that don't make sense to me. I'm the one that got dumped. He's the one that got Cecile. And he's the one who thinks he has a beef. That make any sense to you?"

Bert thought it over. While he did so, he stroked his dog's head like he was stroking his own chin in contemplation. The dog was a rescued chihuahua mutt, not exactly brown, not exactly gray, with enormous bulging eyes and tremendous ears that could pivot to almost any angle. His name was Nacho. He weighed about four pounds and lay in his master's lap like a warm loaf of bread. After one final scratch, the old man said, "No, it don't really make a lotta sense. But since when does jealousy make sense?"

The question hung for a moment in the humid air. On the sidewalk below the bar's raised deck, a flock of drunken bachelorettes wobbled past on ankle-breaking shoes. A man walked by with a cockatoo on his head and a towel full of guano on his shoulder. A woman at his side was cuddling a ferret. They were holding hands like teenagers.

"Anyway," said Sonny, "it was Citarella who got me roped into the stupid hot dog business. Got me in trouble wit' my bookie. The hot dog wagon was my only way out."

Bert scratched Nacho. "'Scuse me, Sonny, but maybe I'm missin' a connection heah. Like between the bookie and the hot dog."

"Well, it's a little bit complicated story. Got time for another drink?"

By way of answer, the old man gestured to the bartender for a fresh round. There was an elegant economy in how he did this, a self-assured mastery that could only come from many years of practice. A lift of a finger and a slight nod of the head was all it took.

"So ya see," Sonny went on, "where it starts, well, I'm a guy that likes to gamble. It's a weakness. I admit it. But I enjoy it. What can I say? It gives me a thrill. And I'm a very loyal guy. Another weakness, I guess. A loyal guy from Brooklyn. So who do I bet on? The hometown teams, of course. The Mets. The Jets. The Giants. The Knicks. Problem is, they all stink. They always lose."

"So why not bet onna Yankees?" Bert put in.

"I hate the Yankees. What the fuck fun is it to bet on a team that always wins?"

"I guess that's one waya lookin' at it."

"So anyway, a coupla years ago I get on a really lousy losing streak. Name a sport, I lose money on it. The spread is three, my guys lose by four. The spread is four, they lose by five. Ya know how it is. And the whole time, Citarella keeps eggin' me on. *It's gotta turn,* he says. *Double down,* he says. And meanwhile, he keeps gettin' me more credit. Like he's doin' me a favor."

"Ah," said Bert, "so he's like your...what the hell's that word? Enacter? Engager? Disabler? Somethin' like that."

"Well, anyway, I'm down a hundred grand before I get it through my head that I might really be fuckin' myself wit' this. I mean, I know how it works. I know what happens to guys who fall too far behind. I've seen it. Up close. So now I'm worried. Maybe even scared, ya want the truth. And my good pal Citarella keeps the spigot open, and then finally, when I'm in the toilet for a hundred and a quarter, he changes his tune and starts reminding me that I'm in big trouble but that maybe, if he were to help me out, if he were to stick his neck out for me, well, maybe somethin' could be worked out."

The fresh drinks arrived. Bert lifted the maraschino cherry from his Old-Fashioned and briefly dangled it above the dog. The dog shot up from his lap like a bonefish taking a fly and bit off the ersatz fruit precisely at the stem, then immediately settled back into its contented stupor in its master's crotch. The old man said, "So this somethin' that could be worked out—"

"Right," said Sonny, slurping on his vodka and lime. "So he sets up a meet with the Big Guy."

"Fat Lou?" said Bert, unable to hide that he was surprised and impressed.

"Fat Lou himself."

"I see. So this Citarella might be a prick and a hypocrite but at least he's got the right connections."

"Yeah, he does," conceded Sonny. "Prob'ly part of the reason Cecile dumped me for him. Bettin' on a winner. What a concept, huh? Anyway, so I drive into the City and go to his club—"

"He still down on Sullivan Street?"

"Yeah. So you know the place?"

"Like my own livin' room. Three steps down from the sidewalk. The espresso machine. The pool table. Then ya got the curtain into the room where the goombahs watch TV. Then another curtain where Fat Lou sits and eats."

"Yeah, that's how it was. In fact he was eatin' when I got there."

"Don't surprise me. He's always eatin'. What was he havin'?"

"A calzone. Big fuckin' calzone. I mean that fuckin' calzone was bigger than your dog. 'Cept it was cut in half. Cut in half and still had the silver foil on it. Cheese was oozin' outa the cut end. Fat Lou kinda chased the cheese around with his tongue the whole time he was talkin' to me. Chase some cheese, nibble off a little crust, chase cheese again. I gotta say it wasn't pretty."

"Disgustin' table manners Fat Lou has. Like an animal he eats. So anyway, this thing ya worked out—"

"This is what I'm gettin' to. So he starts in remindin' me how much I'm in hock for, and how at the rate I'm goin' I'll never get my head above water, and that's really a shame 'cause people can't just go around lettin' debts slide, 'cause otherwise where would we be? So, bottom line, there has to be repayment. Then he raises a finger, very philosophical like, and says but maybe the repayment don't have to be in cash. Maybe there's a way to work off what you owe.

"So now he's got me in suspense. Like, work it off, how? Is he gonna make me take a contract on some poor shnook? Ice somebody? Hurt somebody? That ain't me, Bert. I hate that shit. So I'm waitin' to hear what he's gonna say, and meantime he goes back to the calzone. Nibblin' crust, chasin' cheese. And I'm thinkin' about how stupid it was to bet on the Giants and the Jets and what the hell am I gonna do if it comes down to a choice where either I off some other loser or I get offed myself. I mean this is where the rubber meets the road, right? Am I gonna get punished or is my punishment gonna be that I gotta punish some other poor bastard? So I'm wrestlin' wit' my conscience while Fat Lou finishes the first halfa the calzone, crumples up the silver foil, and pushes it off the edge of the table onto the floor."

"Just like that? No gahbidge can?"

"No can."

"Guy's a pig. How the hell was he brought up?"

"Well, anyway, he wipes his mouth on his handkerchief, picks a couple teeth with a fingernail, and tells me that what he wants me to do, which by the way is a forgiveness and opportunity I should be grateful for, is really very simple. He wants me to move to Key West and run a hot dog truck. Unnerstand, in that moment I can hardly believe my ears. I can hardly believe I'm gettin' off so easy. No baseball bats, no .38s. Just run a hot dog truck."

"'Cept I'm guessin' there was a catch," Bert put in.

"Well, yeah, sure. Course there was. The hot dog truck was gonna be a drop."

"A drop for what?"

"Well, that's what I asked too," said Sonny. "Only natural, right? 'Cept Fat Lou don't answer the question.

What he does instead is he picks up the second halfa the calzone and starts peelin' down the foil a little bit so he can start lickin' at the cheese again. Then he asks me how my geography is. 'My geography?' I say. 'I know which bridge to take to Staten Island and how to get to Jersey. Other than that, I ain't got no geography.' So he launches into this whole spiel about what an amazing spot Key West is in. Water all around that connects it to the whole resta the world by boat. A dinky airport wit' shit security that connects it by air. A road fulla tourists that connects it by car. So let's say a guy slips in by a small boat from the Caymans or Bahamas or pretty much anywhere and goes out for a hot dog. Who's gonna notice? Who's gonna care? Say a day or so later a different guy comes in for a hot dog before flyin' to New York or drivin' to Miami. What's special about that? Who's gonna put these guys together? Who's gonna suspect? It's just a fuckin' hot dog truck next to a beach. Perfect for a drop."

Bert rattled the shrinking ice cubes in his half-empty glass. "I get that part. I get it. But a drop for what? This is what I'm askin'."

Somewhat sheepishly, Sonny said, "I have no idea."

"No idea?"

"None. Look, Fat Lou tells me from the start that I don't need to know what's in the packages. It's safer I don't know, he says. They're packaged up just so. Anything's messed wit', tampered wit', I'm in deep shit. Very deep. Do I understand? So I say fine, I don't need to know. What else could I say?"

"You weren't curious?"

"Course I was. Who wouldn't be? But I'd rather be curious than dead."

"Hm," said Bert. He rubbed his dog and looked out at the sidewalk. It was one of those odd moments in a Duval Street evening when the town seemed to be getting quieter and noisier all at once. The rumble of traffic subsided just as the music was cranking up in the bars; the wind dropped just as the raucous laughing and occasional screaming matches started blowing harder; there was a kind of crazy balance to it. "So how long did you have to do this?"

"Well, that's another thing Fat Lou wouldn't answer. 'Until the debt's paid off,' he says. So I'm thinkin' what the fuck does that mean? Six months? A year? The resta my life? But let's face it, I got no leverage to negotiate. Anyway, Fat Lou puts the calzone down for about five seconds and says, 'Look, you do your job, I'll treat ya fair. When it's enough, it's enough. You'll know. We got a deal?' So we shake on it, and that's that."

"And that was, what, about two years ago?"

"Comin' up on. So I fly to Miami to pick up the wagon and get more skinny about how the whole thing's gonna work, and guess who's there to meet me?"

"How the fuck should I know?"

"Take a guess."

"Okay. Al Pacino."

"Al Pacino? Why the hell would Al Pacino meet me in Miami?"

"I have no idea. Ya told me take a guess. It's the first name that popped inta my head."

"Well, it was Citarella."

"Citarella? Ah, maybe I shoulda figured. But I thought he was a New York guy."

"He was. He is. He's both. Ya see, he's smart. It kills me t'admit it, but it's true. He's a mover. Cecile saw that right away. His potential, I mean. S'anyway, he manages to make himself sorta the go-between between Fat Lou and this Miami boss—"

"Ya mean Charlie Ponte by any chance?"

"Ponte, yeah. That's the guy. Ya know him?"

"Only for half a century or so. We been friends. We been enemies. Almost killed each other once or twice. I guess ya could sorta say we run the gamut, whatever the hell a gamut is. You got any idea what a gamut is?"

"Not really, no. But anyway, it turns out Cecile wanted all along to move to Florida, which she always used to talk about, even back when she was wit' me, but I couldn't see my way clear to make it happen. Citarella could. He made some connections so he could be sort of half-time in Miami, and stash Cecile there so she'd be happy and get off his back about wantin' to move, and meantime still take care of business in New York. Which meant that he was practically my boss on the hot dog thing, which sorta stuck in my craw because now, on toppa takin' Cecile away from me, he's painted me into a corner where I'm sweatin' bullets over a hot griddle while he's pursuin' career advancement all up and down the whole east coast while also sippin' highballs wit' Cecile in air-conditioned comfort. Does that seem fair to you?"

Bert drained his drink. A squad of Harleys roared down the street in tight formation, piloted by men with silver ponytails, sleeveless denim vests with silver studs, low-slung jeans that showed the uppermost half-inch of their butt-cracks. Probably dentists and accountants when they weren't on vacation. When the popping razz of their engines had died down, the old man said, "Nah, it don't seem fair. It seems like life. But, ya know, it always kinda struck me that you enjoyed the hot dog job."

Sonny ran a hand through his thick black hair and couldn't help half-smiling. "Well, parts of it I kinda did, that's the crazy part. I mean, it was pretty low-stress mosta the time. If business was slow, I'd mostly stand there lookin' at the ocean, the women onna beach. Got to kibitz with the regulars. Got to give away a lotta food, which I enjoyed. I mean, free food makes people happy, right, and it's not like anyone was keepin' inventory onna French fries. So it wasn't bad. But I didn't love not knowin' what I was inna middle of."

"Wit' the drop, ya mean?"

"Yeah. Wit' the drop. But it's not like it was an every day thing or anything like that."

"So how'd it work?" Bert asked.

Sonny looked around in all directions before lowering his chin and voice to answer. "Different ways different times. Ya see, I'd never know when a drop was coming. Sometimes it might be once a week, other times more like once a month. And there were different guys who made the drops. Sometimes it would be a black guy with an accent from the islands. Sometimes it would be a white guy who looked like he just stepped off a yacht. Prob'ly half a dozen different guys altogether. So I never knew. So there had to be a code. A password, like. So the guy would have to come up to the window and say, 'Gimme a burnt one, ketchup onna roll, mustard onna dog, cut the pickle sideways.'"

"Cut the pickle sideways?"

"Yeah. That's what made it foolproof. I mean, who's gonna ask for that? So anyway, the guy would hand me a little box—"

"How little?"

Sonny gestured with his giant hands. "Little. Like it coulda held, hell, I don't know, like half a dozen bon-bons."

Bert petted the dog. "Bon-bons?"

"Ya know, those little chocolates. Almonds or coconut or some shit. Just, like, from the drugstore. Nothin' fancy. Useta pick 'em up for Cecile alla time. Justa let 'er know I'm thinkin' about her. She'd eat 'em in fronta television. Six chocolates. Anyway, the boxes were about that size. So I'd take 'em, wait till no one else was at the window, then stick 'em in this little hidey-hole we had, this secret spot in the drawer that held the buns. Then, a day or two later, sometimes longer, another guy would show up, more a Brooklyn kinda guy, say the abracadabra pickle thing, I'd hand him the package, and that was that. Pretty simple really. Or pretty simple till a couple months ago."

"'Zat when ya closed up the wagon?" Bert asked. "I remember bein' a little bit surprised. Thought maybe ya were sick or somethin', takin' some vacation maybe. But then it didn't open up no more and started gettin' all plastered over wit' the violation stickers."

"Well, what happened," Sonny said, "is that one day I get a call from Citarella and he's tellin' me to shut it down. Just outa the blue. Shut it down. I ask him why. He tells me because there's too much heat on. This was news to me. I ask him where the heat is comin' from. Local cops? Feds? Competitors? Who? He doesn't tell me nothin', just says shut it down. This puts me in an awkward spot. I mean, my deal was wit' Fat Lou, so I tell Citarella that I'd be more comfortable hearin' from Lou direct that the job was over and I didn't have to do it no more. He gets kinda huffy, like I just gave him some kinda insult or somethin', and tells me, look, he's tryin' to do me a favor, which by the way is what he always tells me when he's pullin' me deeper inta somethin' where I end up gettin' screwed. He says it's fine wit' Fat Lou, I can take his word for that, and that I should get the hell outa town and go back to New York. I tell him there's just one slight problem wit' that. There was a drop the day before yesterday that hasn't been picked up yet. It's sittin' in there wit' the buns. He acts like he knew that all along, which maybe he did or maybe he didn't. Who knows wit' him? Anyway, he tells me don't worry about it, it'll get picked up when the heat is off. Just shut it down, he tells me. He'll handle it. So, stupid me, I do like he says, even though I sorta know deep down, kinda the way ya know deep down when you've made a losin' bet, that there's gonna come a time when that last drop comes back to bite me innee ass."

"Which I gather," said Bert, "is what has now transpired, or to put it in what you might call a more biblical way that would suggest the deeper workings of fate, come to pass."

It took Sonny a moment to unravel the phrasing. While he was working on it, Bert signaled for one more round of drinks. Why not? By Key West time, it was early yet. There hadn't yet been any brawls. No sirens, no nearby tables tipping over.

"Come to pass and then some," the younger man said at last. "So what happened is that a coupla days ago I get another call from Citarella. I'm back in Brooklyn, y'unnerstand, thinkin' everything is hunky-dory and I'm home free wit' the hot dog business. I mean, it's been weeks since I even thought about it. Well, he gets real serious onna phone and tells me we got a problem. I'm thinkin', wait a second, *we* got a problem? What's this *we* shit, kemosabe? Anyway, he tells me that Ponte, the Miami guy, is up his ass about that last drop that didn't get picked up, and he wants some fuckin' answers. I say to him, Frankie, what's to answer? I told you there was one more package. You told me there was too much heat, let it sit, leave town, you'd handle it.

"So whaddya think he has the balls to say to me then? He says, 'I never told you that.' I say, 'Yeah, you did. That's exactly what you told me.' He says, 'No it ain't. I told you finish the job.'"

"So look, I guess I'm a little slow onnee uptake, but by now I'm startin' to figure out what's goin' on here. Namely, Citarella's screwin' me again. He gave me wrong advice, now I'm gettin' blamed for takin' it. Plus he talks to the big guys direct, and I don't. Plus everybody thinks he's so goddamn smart. Who're they gonna think remembers things better? Plus, let's face it, I was the hot dog guy, not him. So all in all I'm screwed. So I say to him, Frankie, this ain't fair and you know it ain't fair, but okay, ya got me, wha' do I gotta do? He says get your ass down to Key West right away and open up the truck again and keep it open till the pick-up's made.

"Now, I'm in Brooklyn, remember. He's already in Florida. For about half a second, I think why the hell doesn't *he* go open up the hot dog truck? Then it hits me like a pinch inna nuts. He wouldn't do it 'cause it's beneath his dignity. He's gotten way too big for that. There's guys that call the shots and there's guys that sweat the hot dogs. No wonder Cecile went wit' him. So anyway, and let's face it, it's not like

I had anything that special goin' on in New York anyway, I get inna car and drive to Key West. I get here very late last night. What's the first thing I do? Go over to the hot dog. I see the truck, right where it was two months ago. Fine. But before I can go in, I see a cat. A cat I recognize. Wanderin' around at three, four inna morning. So I'm concerned. So the cat comes right over to me and I see where it lives from the tag. So I think the right thing to do would be to bring it home. So I drive it to the address, chat a few minutes wit' this very nice lady whose cat it is, and then guess what? By the time I get back to the hot dog truck, the fucking thing is gone."

"Gone?"

"Gone."

"Gone where?"

"Fuck if I know."

"Hm," said Bert, and fed the third whisky-soaked cherry to his now wobbly dog. "Ya know, when I went down to the beach this morning, I thought somethin' looked different, but I couldn't put my finger on what it was. Funny, ain't it, how that works? I mean, the food trucks are practically right outside my front door, right across the street from my condo. So I look at the lineup every single day for years and years, then part of it all of a sudden disappears and I couldn't quite tell what's missin'."

"Well, what's gonna be missin' is my ass if I can't find the hot dog and get that last drop taken care of. That's why I called ya, Bert. I could really use some help."

At that the old man firmed up his posture and gave a light tug to the placket of his lavender silk shirt. These were the sorts of moments, increasingly rare from year to year, that he lived for; these opportunities to help a friend, a colleague, or even a total stranger; to get involved with something big or at least different; to stick his nose into someone else's business and have something to do other than walk the dog, watch the sun go down, and now and then play gin rummy. Graciously, he said, "Well, sure, Sonny. Happy to help if I can. So where do things stand as of this moment?"

"Well, where they stand is that the hot dog is AWOL and I don't know who took it or if anybody else knows yet that it's missing."

"You didn't tell Citarella?"

"Nah, I figured he would freak. Besides, I thought it would be better not to show my cards. I mean, I don't really trust the guy."

"I've kinda picked up on that."

"I mean, what if he took the thing himself? That would be just like Citarella. Puts me inna middle. Tells the bosses I'm comin' down to handle the pick-up. Last second, wit' me in town, now the hot dog and the package disappear. Who's gonna get the blame? Me. Who's gonna get the package? Him."

"But you got no idea what's in the package. Does he?"

"I don't know if he knows or doesn't know. Nobody tells me nothin'."

"And you got no proof he took it."

"No, I don't. None at all. It's just a hunch. But why the hell would anybody else bother to steal a beat-up old hot dog wagon?"

"Hm," said Bert, and scratched the dog's head, though the dog had either gone to sleep or passed out in his lap. The little creature wheezed softly as it slept, its ears twitching randomly. "Well, offhand, or off the cuff, or off the toppa my head, it seems to me ya got two choices. Either ya find the hot dog—"

"Which could be fuckin' anywhere," Sonny interrupted, his frustration finally bubbling over. "Could be in Miami by now for all I know. Or maybe Citarella scored the package and had the wagon sunk to the bottom a the ocean. How the fuck am I supposed to find it?"

Very calmly, Bert said, "Which brings us to the second choice, which, judgin' by your little outburst, I would observe or guess to be your preference. Maybe I can set up a meet wit' Ponte, and you and me and Citarella can all sit down like grownups and try in a calm and grownup way to figure out what's what wit' this elusive hot dog so that no one gets screwed if in fact he didn't do somethin' very wrong that would deserve a screwin'."

"You can do that, Bert? You can get it so I can talk direct to Ponte?"

"I think so. Worth a try."

"Man, thanks a million. You're a prince."

"Not really. Just a guy who's been around the block a couple times. *Salud.*"

They clinked their nearly empty glasses. Down on the street, someone screamed like he was being stabbed then laughed like a hyena. A pink Cadillac convertible crawled by with three drag beauty queens sitting high up on the boot and blowing kisses.

Sonny drained his vodka then said a little sheepishly, "Bert, I hate t'ask, but can I ask ya one more favor? I'm sorta flat dead broke."

"Hey, no problem. Drinks on me. Ya need some cash? I happen to have a little extra beyond my modest needs."

"Thanks. Thanks a lot. I'll pay ya back."

Or not, the old man thought. Whatever.

"And, um, maybe one more thing," Sonny went on. "If I'm not pushin' my luck here."

"Go 'head, push it. I like your style."

"Well, I could really use a place to stay. After tonight, I mean."

"Where ya stayin' tonight?"

"The people wit' the cat. The wife invited me. Nice place. Over on Poorhouse Lane."

"Wait a sec," said Bert. "Poorhouse Lane. Fancy cat. We talkin' the Kaplans by any chance?"

"I don't know their last name. Meg and Peter."

Bert stroked the comatose chihuahua and riffled through his memory. "Shit, I'm not so good wit' names these days. But the Kaplans, she's very sweet and maybe a little bit woo-woo, kinda out there, truth be told, and he's a nervous guy, kinda jumpy, little bit neurotic maybe, worries about everything."

"Tha'd be them."

"Whaddya know. Small world. Small island, at least. Well, give 'em my regards. An' if ya wanna room wit' me awhile, you're welcome to the couch. Kind of a perfect vantage point to observe or even do some let's say discreet surveillance of what goes on at the beach and by the food trucks and so forth. We can kinda keep an eye out, see if anything suspicious is goin' on over there. Ya know, anything outa the ordinary or let's just say not normal."

6

It was after midnight by the time Peter, lying dressed and sleepless next to his serenely sleeping wife, finally heard the front door of his house open and close. Breathlessly, he listened to Sonny's heavy tread on the stairs that led up to the guest room. In the slightly spectral quiet of the neighborhood around the cemetery, he could hear the splash of his visitor's peeing, the rasp of his gargling, the final spit of toothpaste in the sink. Not until he'd heard the song of the bedsprings as they settled under Sonny's bulk did he slip out from underneath the sheet, grab his car key, and slink away to warn Piney and Fred that the man whose hot dog wagon they'd innocently taken was back in town and apparently inclined to beat them to a pulp.

He wove through narrow residential streets to the ocean. Along the A1A, starlight was twinkling on the low but choppy waves and the palms were gently swaying in perfect parallels, like the backup singers in a Motown group. The air smelled of squeezed limes and damp shells left behind by the tide. Beyond the airport, where the road curved left and was bounded by the Cow Key Channel, the mangroves thickened and Peter noted with relief that the hot dog van was virtually invisible through the tangled and engulfing foliage. Then again, the moon had set and it was very dark; at first he couldn't even find the narrow bumpy track that the wagon had followed from the roadway to the snug and secret clearing.

At length, he saw the beaten path and pulled off onto the weedy shoulder. Before getting out of the car, he checked his side- and rear-view mirrors to make sure he wasn't being tailed; he'd seen people do that often in the movies and it seemed like a prudent maneuver now. Then, stubbing his toes against unseen roots and coral nubs, he made his way slowly into the mangroves.

The outside world vanished almost instantly under the low canopy of intertwining twigs and leaves. Sounds were soft but uncannily distinct. Geckos scuffled in the underbrush. Tree toads bleated like tiny sheep. Not far away, somebody was snoring.

Up ahead, not more than thirty yards from the road and the whole world it connected to, the hot dog wagon sat so snugly perched in its clearing that it might have been dropped from the sky and the mangrove forest long ago grown up around it. The red frankfurter on top looked a very dull brown in the darkness. The yellow mustard squiggle caught occasional pinpricks of starlight. The service window was wide open in the mild weather, as if the vending wagon was open for business but all its customers had been transferred to some other universe.

Peter edged his way closer. The snoring got louder. Finally he was near enough to see Pineapple and Fred laid out between the griddle and the dormant fridge. Piney's head was by Fred's bare feet; Fred's face was close to Piney's toes. Their bedrolls were discreetly separated by a tightly folded blanket. Their pillows were their extra shirts. Fred was the one who was snoring; it was not a steady, rhythmic kind of snore. It had pauses and catches; you couldn't tell where the accent would fall.

For a moment Peter watched them sleep, then said, "Psssst."

Fred suddenly sat bolt upright and in half a second his machete was in his hand and raised above his head like a samurai sword.

Pineapple, still apparently asleep, made a comforting gesture toward Fred's shoulder and murmured, "It's okay, Fred. It's just a dream."

Peter said, "No. It isn't just a dream. It's me. Peter. Can you please put the machete down?"

By then, Pineapple was sitting up as well, the two of them yawning and stretching between the long-dry sink and the drawer still filled with moldy buns. Casually, without panic, as if nothing surprised him anymore and a late night visitor greeting him through a hot dog service window in a mangrove clearing was neither more nor less than normal, he said, "Oh, hi, Peter. What's up?"

"Well, um, we sort of seem to have a problem. Can we talk?"

So the two men, shirtless and in frayed cutoffs, clambered up from the floor and out the back door of the hot dog and they all sat down on the coral rocks that ringed the remains of their campfire. Fred said, "Wanna beer?"

Peter said, "No, no thanks...Well, sure, what the hell, why not?"

Fred grabbed two cans from the cooler. They weren't cool anymore. Pineapple drank water from a scratched up old canteen.

"Well, I don't exactly know how to tell you this," the visitor went on, "but, well, Sonny's back in town."

Pineapple said, "Hot dog Sonny? The guy who owns it?"

"Or used to own it," Fred put in. "Or thinks he owns it."

Peter sucked some warm beer and eventually brought himself to swallow it. "Actually, he says he doesn't own it. What he says is that he's in charge of it, responsible."

"Okay then," Fred said with satisfaction, "if he doesn't own it—"

"Well, look, whether he owns it or not, the problem is that he's a big strong guy who's very pissed off that someone took it, and if he finds out it was you, and with me tagging along, well, I'm a little afraid we'll all end up in the hospital."

"The hospital?" said Piney, and he shivered. "I was in there once. Didn't like the way they looked at me. Didn't like it at all."

Fred said, a little bit suspiciously, "And how you know all this? That's he's back in town, I mean, and what the deal is on the wagon."

"Well, this is kind of weird, totally unplanned, but he's staying at my house."

"At your house?" said Piney.

"Look, my wife invited him. She's very nice to everyone. She just can't help it. Just can't wait to help people out. Always on the lookout for old ladies who fell down, some blind guy crossing three blocks away. Drives me nuts sometimes. Anyway, what happened, well...Sonny happens to come back from Brooklyn late last night. He's heading to the wagon just when I'm out looking for the cat. But he finds the cat before I do, so he brings it home."

"To *his* home?" asked Pineapple.

"No, to my home. I don't think he even has a home down here. Not anymore at least. So he brings the cat to my house, which makes my wife think he's basically a nice guy. That he took the trouble, I mean. Also, my wife thinks he's probably okay because the cat seems to like him. She's sort of a Buddhist."

"The cat's a Buddhist?" said Fred.

"Not the cat. My wife. My wife's a Buddhist. Why do you keep mixing up the cat and my wife? Anyway, my wife's kind of a Buddhist and she seems to think the cat's got some kind of mystic power that makes her this great judge of character. I don't happen to agree. I think it's more about the French fries. But anyway, this is what she thinks."

Fred said, "Well, I'm glad we cleared up who's the Buddhist, but I still don't understand why he's staying at your house."

"Well, okay, so he brings the cat home, and in the meantime, that's when you guys roll away the hot dog with me inside. So he comes back to the beach. Suddenly no hot dog. He's understandably bewildered and very upset. So he goes back to my place because it's very late and he has nowhere else to go, and my wife offers him to spend the night. So I talk to him earlier today—"

"At your house," said Fred.

"Correct. Out by the pool."

"You have a pool?" said Pineapple.

Peter instantly wished he hadn't said it. He didn't want to be one of those people who has to work it into every conversation that he has a swimming pool. "Just a small one. Nothing fancy."

"It have a diving board?"

"No. Too shallow."

"I once rolled off a diving board back when I was drinking."

"Piney, fuck the diving board and let him get to the important part. S'okay, you're talking with him at your house. By the pool, or the cabana, or the lanai—"

"We don't have a lanai. Anyway, he's very upset and he starts talking in his Brooklyn kind of way about all the bad things that should happen to the knees and teeth of people who mess with other people's vending wagons, so I start getting pretty nervous and tell a fib or two like I don't know anything about it. But then he starts telling me about how *he's* in trouble, big trouble, and he thinks somebody named Citarella probably took the hot dog and is trying to set him up. You follow me?"

"Um, not really," said Pineapple. "I mean, I get it that

maybe we're in trouble. But why's he in trouble?"

"Well, I don't know exactly, and maybe I just worry too much. That's what my wife says, that I worry too much, even about things with just the tiniest little chance of going wrong. Which, by the way, they often do, no matter what she says. But anyway, here's what I can't help thinking. Sonny's talking broken knees, knocked out teeth. Now there's this mystery man Citarella who he thinks is trying to set him up for something. Am I just getting panicky, or does this sound a little bit like, well, a little bit like Mafia?"

"Mafia?" said Fred, almost spitting out some beer. "Come on, dude, I think you've watched too many movies out on your lanai."

"I just told you I don't have a lanai."

"We're in fuckin' Key West, man. What's the Mafia want with Key West? The Mafia's in the hot dog business?"

"Look, I don't know. All I know is that, as things now stand, we're in trouble with Sonny, and Sonny is in trouble with someone else, and that someone else might possibly be the Mob. And if we're the reason that Sonny is in trouble with the Mob, then, *ergo*, we'd also be in trouble with the Mob."

Piney said, "Ergo? Who's Ergo?"

"Sorry, forget *ergo*. Bad habit from my professor days. But look, Mafia, no Mafia, we have to get something decided, and right now is our best chance to get it done. It was my wife's idea."

Fred said, "Oh great. The Buddhist."

"She has a very practical side as well. So, look, Sonny's asleep at our house right now. There's no chance he'll be out snooping around. So the question is, do we put the hot dog back, act like none of this ever happened, and hope he never figures it out? Or do you guys keep the hot dog, hope he doesn't find it, and hope the whole thing just blows over, which, who knows, maybe it will? It's your place. It really needs to be your decision."

Pineapple looked at Fred. Fred looked at the ground. Crickets rasped. Frogs let out belching croaks.

After a long moment, Piney said, "Well, I hate to say it, but I guess we gotta put it back."

"Why?" said Fred. "Why the hell should we put it back? It's ours as much as Sonny's. He said he doesn't own it, right?"

"Well, but neither do we. And he had it first."

"Yeah, and he let it get all covered over with violation stickers and then he walked away. And now we have it. So it goes."

"I don't know, Fred. It just doesn't feel right. Guy's never done us any harm. Doesn't feel right we'd be getting him in trouble."

"He got himself in trouble."

"Someone gets in trouble," Piney argued mildly, "it's not always their fault."

"Well, it's sure as hell not our fault."

Piney just shrugged at that. "Besides," he said, "the way I see it, we slept on the ground two nights ago, we'll sleep on the ground tomorrow. We won't be any the worse off."

Fred blinked up at the hot dog and wiped his mouth with the back of his hand. The pride of ownership that he'd felt the night before was fading now to a kind of nostalgia in advance, as if he was already thinking back to the good old days, of which there had been exactly one. "No worse off?" he said. "I guess. But it's sure as shit gonna feel like we are."

He drained his beer, slapped his hands onto his knees, and pushed himself up from the rock he'd been sitting on. "But okay," he went on, "no use keeping it if we're gonna feel bad about it. If we're gonna give 'er back, let's get it the hell over with."

The others also rose, and for a minute or two they walked around the hot dog with their chins in their hands, considering it from every angle, appraising the geometry of the task before them. Maneuvering the wagon into the snug clearing had been a near-herculean labor, but lightened by excitement and a sense of expanding possibilities. Getting it out again would be even tougher, the work now made bitter by the taint of capitulation and defeat. Smacking a mosquito on the back of his neck, Fred said, "S'gonna be a bear getting 'er turned around."

"We can do it," Piney said.

Fred took another lap around the site. "Maybe we don't need to jackass it all the way, at least."

He asked Peter if he'd come up by car. Peter said he had.

"Got a hitching ball on it?"

"What's a hitching ball?"

"Guess that means you don't. Two kinds of people in the world. Those with hitches on their vehicles and those without. Well, maybe we can manage with a rope. Okay with you to give us a tow?"

Peter was dubious, worried, of course, about anything that had even the tiniest little chance of going wrong, but felt that, under the circumstances, he could hardly say no. So, while Piney and Fred were gathering up their few things from inside the hot dog, he left the clearing and walked the thirty yards or so of rooty, rutted path that led back to the road. He got in his car, took a couple deep breaths and a careful look around, then spun the steering wheel and started backing very slowly into the tunnel of encroaching mangroves. Stiff branches clawed at his paint job and snapped against his side-view mirrors. Smears of sap and tatters of leaf befouled his windshield. Springs groaned over roots and the chassis scraped against a coral slab. The bouncing made his eyeballs ache and he realized he'd better not go any farther.

He stopped and tried to get out of the car but couldn't open the door against the pressure of the foliage; his claustrophobia kicked in and made him picture distressing news footage featuring the jaws of life. He rolled down his window and a spider web pasted itself against his nose. He called out to Fred to ask how it was going with the rope.

"Great, just peachy. Piney's underneath the hot dog, tying it onto the frame. We'll be ready in a minute. Just sit tight."

So he sat there, very tight. He took deep breaths. The mangroves in front of him gobbled up the brightness of his headlights and sent back only a morbid glare. He started to sweat. He wished he'd brought his panic pills.

Finally, Fred appeared in the rear-view mirror, squatted down, and tied the rope around his bumper. In the confident voice of a foreman, he said, "Okay now, nice and easy. Steady on the gas. Slow and steady."

Peter put the car in gear and edged forward till the slack was out of the rope. Then he made a foot or so of creaking, labored progress before the movement just stopped dead. He fed more gas; the engine revved but the load went nowhere.

Fred called out, "Whoa, whoa," and went to investigate.

His report was that the car was hung up on a root, the hot dog was hung up on a rock, and that this was going to be the hard part but then it would get way easier.

Peter doubted that but managed a good-sport sort of smile and kept adding to the weight on the accelerator. The engine hummed, then whined, then roared. The car shook from side to side but stayed right where it was.

So he squeezed the steering wheel, locked his elbows, tightened down his jaw, and floored it.

The stymied vehicle rocked, teetered, hesitated, then all of a sudden the resistance was gone and it jetted forward, scraping and clattering wildly through the shrubbery and over the stony ground until it came skidding and shrieking to a sideways halt just shy of the roadway.

Shaking and pale, Peter got of the car and tried to figure what had happened. He walked to the rear of the vehicle and saw that the rope was no longer attached. Neither was the bumper. Where it had been, there was a neat rectangular indentation, as from a skin graft, and a series of square holes in the body.

He picked his way back down the path through a chaos of snapped twigs and broken branches. About twenty yards in, he saw his bumper on the ground, still attached to the rope like some failed and monstrous kite.

Ahead, in the clearing, he saw the hot dog, maybe two feet from where it had been, but now leaning at a jaunty angle, so that one corner rested on the ground and the frankfurter on top sort of looked like it was poised for takeoff.

"Axle busted," Fred explained tersely as Peter moved in for a closer look. "Too much torque. That last pull done 'er in. Guess she ain't going nowhere now."

Pineapple said, "Guess we shoulda just drug 'er back by hand. Same way we got 'er here. That worked okay."

"I didn't hear you suggesting that before," Fred pointed out.

"I figured you knew best," said Piney.

"Well, anyway," his pal went on, "water under the bridge. Neither here nor there. Point is, we tried to give 'er back. We gave it our best shot. It didn't work out. So be it. My conscience is clear."

"Mine isn't."

"Christ, Piney, we tried."

"Right. And Sonny's still in trouble 'cause of us."

"Look," Fred said, "you can't spend your whole life worrying about other people's problems."

"You know, I say that same thing to my wife sometimes," Peter put in.

"There, ya see, Piney, even the professor with the swimming pool agrees with me."

"Now wait a sec. I didn't say that. I'm not taking sides here. In fact, all in all, I think things would've been simpler if we gave it back."

"Oh, so now you're taking *his* side?"

"Look, I just said I wasn't taking either side. I'm just...well, I'm just very, very tired and a little bit freaked about being trapped inside my car, and aside from that, I'm a little bit upset about my bumper."

"Ah, they'll stick it back on," said Fred. "Probably cost about the same as the hitching ball woulda. Kind of a wash, really."

"Very comforting," said Peter. "Plus, after all this, now the hot dog's wrecked and isn't any use to you guys anyway."

"Wrecked? Who says it's wrecked? It isn't wrecked. It isn't wrecked at all. You people with houses and lanais. One little thing goes wrong, you think it's wrecked. The hot dog, all it is, it's tilted. We horse it up on a rock, get 'er level, it's good as new, it just won't roll no more."

At that, the sober Piney could not hold back a cockeyed smile and a brief and bashful laugh.

Fred put his hands on his hips and looked impatient. "Okay, Pineapple," he said. "Mister Conscience. Mister Worrying About Other People's Problems. What's so goddamn funny all of a sudden?"

The tall man looked down at the ground and made a modest and disclaiming gesture. "Well, okay, it's kind of dumb, but...won't roll. Get it? It's still a hot dog but now it doesn't have a roll. I mean, I still feel bad about Sonny and all. But what can I say? I just think that's kind of funny."

7

Back on Poorhouse Lane, the night air was fragrant with lemon blossoms and jasmine, the palm fronds made a lulling sound like softly played maracas, and Meg was sleeping in the exact same position she'd been in when Peter had slipped out of bed a couple of hours before. It was uncanny how peacefully she slept; it was a miracle of calm and trust.

Her husband sat down lightly next to her and touched her on the shoulder. She didn't stir. He gave her a little shake. She softly said *hmmm?* Then she raised her head a few inches from the pillow, wiped away a damp spot where she'd slobbered a little, and said, "Oh, hi, honey. How'd it go?"

"Badly."

"Oh, I'm sorry."

"The hot dog's leaning over and the bumper got yanked off the car. I stuck it in the trunk. It's sort of folded down the middle."

Sleepily, she said, "So you didn't get it moved? The hot dog? You didn't put it back?"

"I thought I just explained that, Meg. No, we didn't put it back. The whole thing was a fiasco, a disaster. The car is beat to shit. The hot dog has a broken axle. We couldn't get it moved. No one will ever get it moved. It'll remain in place, *in situ*, forever and all time. It'll be a monument, a ruin, a tourist attraction, a mystery for future civilizations to try to figure out what the hell it was. That hot dog isn't going anywhere. That hot dog is stuck."

"Oh well," Meg said serenely, "Anyway, the way I see it, things end up where they're meant to be."

"Oh, is that how you see it? You know, I had a funny feeling that's how you'd see it. In fact, I would have bet my left ball that's how you'd see it." He jerked his thumb in the general direction of the guestroom. "But meanwhile, we have this tough-guy stranger in the house who's very pissed off about the wagon that now can't ever be put back, and I had a claustrophobia attack and the car is trashed, and I'm wondering what your karma coach would say about what I did to end up smack dab in the middle of this cluster-fuck."

"You sound a little agitated, honey."

"Oh, I do?" He drummed his fingers on the yielding mattress and looked around the moonlit room, then said, "Where's the cat?"

Meg moved her feet beneath the light blanket, unsuccessfully searching for Sasha with her toes. "Guess she slipped out when you left. I thought I heard her meowing outside Sonny's door."

"Sonny's door? Meowing? Begging to be let in? That's the last straw. That's really it. Listen, Meg, first thing tomorrow morning, that guy is out of here. I can't take it anymore. I just can't. As of tomorrow, I'm washing my hands of all this craziness. Totally washing my hands."

Calmly, Meg said, "Okay, honey. I think that's a good idea. He'll leave tomorrow after breakfast."

"After breakfast? What is this, a fucking B&B? He has to have French toast first? A veggie omelet maybe? What's next, late check-out, valet parking, little chocolates on the pillow?"

"I just think it would be rude to send a guest away hungry. Goodnight, honey." She raised up higher on an elbow, kissed her husband on the cheek, and instantly went back to sleep.

Peter trudged to the bathroom and took a pill. Then he decided that two would probably be better. He didn't want to have to talk to Sonny in the morning and, for once, he got his wish. He slept till almost noon and when he woke up the visitor had gone.

🏖 🏖 🏖

"Ya see," said Bert the Shirt, cradling his dog to calm him from the rare excitement of a visitor, "from here ya got a whaddyacallit...what's that thing where they charge ya extra for the good seats at the ballgame? A perfectly obstructed view...No, wait, what I think I mean is an unobstructed view. Anyway, check it out."

He put the dog down on the floor, paused briefly for dramatic effect, then swept aside the heavy, sun-faded curtain that covered his third-floor living room window. Below and beyond it, Sonny saw a palm-shaded courtyard with a pool and gazebo and a pair of shuffleboard courts; then the asphalt ribbon of A1A with its usual procession of rented red convertibles and screaming scooters; then the row of vending trucks, now sadly discontinuous in the absence of the hot dog; then the bustling promenade with its veering bikes and wobbly skaters and jaw-clenching joggers determined to stay fit in sheer defiance of the seductive laziness all around them; then the squat limestone complex that held the public restrooms and the outdoor showers; and finally the beach, the twinkling ocean, and the far horizon.

With undisguised pride and pleasure in his privileged perch, the old man went on. "There it is, the whole wide and beautiful world for your perusal and ya might even say delectation, or whatever that long word is when ya really like to look at somethin' and never get sick and tired a lookin' at it just 'cause it's the same thing ya look at every day. This here view, it never gets old. No wonder they call this place the Paradiso."

"Nice," said Sonny, pulling his eyes away from the window to look around the small apartment. It had carpeting that had once been gold but now had dulled to a scuffed brown with pee stains here and there and vaguely faded rectangles where decades of tropical sunshine had leaked through gaps in the curtains. A few chewed-up dog toys were strewn around. A cheeseburger. A pepperoni pizza. A rubber chicken with its head gnawed off.

Nacho was nosing around the toys, seeming hopeful of some playtime, so Sonny squatted down and grabbed the chicken by a leg. The dog sprang over, ears laid back, eyes bulging, toenails hooking their way through carpet loops, and sank its teeth into what was left of the chicken's neck.

"Dog likes ya," Bert observed.

Shrugging modestly while maintaining his grip, Sonny said, "I get along wit' animals. Always have. Dogs. Cats. Never quite knew why."

Bert followed his own line of thought. "If he didn't like ya, ya know what he'd do? He'd pretend to let ya have the fuckin' chicken. He'd act like he didn't even care. Then, first chance, he'd grab the thing and drag it way the hell under the sofa. Why? 'Cause that's his edge. He fits under things. And ya think he doesn't know that that's his edge? Sure he does. Winners always know what their edge is, and they use it. Dog gets ticked off about somethin', he finds somethin' I need. Handkerchief, maybe. Napkin. Somethin' that rolled offa my plate. Whatever. He grabs it and drags it way the hell under the sofa. I spend like twenty minutes tryin' to bend over, another twenty reachin' in and feelin' all around, another twenty tryin' to stand up again. And the whole time, the dog is lookin' at me, smilin'. Like he knows he won. Smart little fucker."

By this time Sonny was rolling on the floor, wrestling with Nacho. The chicken's neck was down to a nub. It had lost one of its yellow feet. From his low angle, the guest looked through a doorway that led into the kitchen and could see a formica dinette with a boomerang pattern and a light fixture that looked like Sputnik. Lifting the chihuahua up onto his chest, he said, "How long ya had the place, Bert?"

"Jeez, must be, what, forty-seven, comin' up on forty-eight years by now."

"Haven't changed it much, I'm guessin'."

"Nah, why would I? Stuff still works. Plus it reminds me of my wife, she should rest in peace. My Rosa. Always cookin' in that little kitchen. Singin' along wit' the radio. Opera mostly. She loved the opera. Very cultured woman, my wife."

He paused. As a token of respect, Sonny stopped roughhousing with the dog and got up from the floor.

"Oh, and that reminds me," Bert went on after the moment of silence. "These might come in handy." He shuffled over to a wobbly end table with a sticking drawer and came out with a tiny pair of binoculars housed in mother-of-pearl. "Her opera glasses. In case ya want a close-up view of any suspicious or let's say possibly un-kosher behavior goin' on inna vicinity of the food trucks. Never know what might crop up."

He handed the miniature binocs to Sonny. They felt fragile as eggshells and faintly ridiculous in his enormous hands and the nosepiece was too narrow to accommodate his flattened schnoz. But he turned back toward the window, held them as close to his eyes as he could manage, and fiddled with the tiny focus rings. Sometimes he saw a single image and sometimes he saw two. Sometimes the image was a circle and sometimes more a sideways figure eight. The crests of wavelets would come into sharp view for a moment but the foreground would be nothing but a blur. Then a palm tree would get sharp but the rest of the world would be just a glaring smudge.

Bert kept right on talking. "Plus," he said, "there's that old sayin' about how the criminal always returns to the scene a the crime. Which, if ya think about it, is pretty fuckin' stupid onna part of the criminal. I mean, say the criminal is you. Why would you return, knowin' that every cop and detective inna world expects you to, like to the point of it bein' a total cliché even, like, on TV and the movies? Like, wait, don't worry, by the third commercial, the criminal will return. Everybody knows it's gotta happen. So if you're the criminal, and unless you're a total fuckin' idiot, why not *not* return for a change? Go somewhere else. Palermo. Jersey City. There's plenty other places ya could go, right?"

Sonny was still messing with the opera glasses, gradually getting a feel for them. He panned across a wide swath of the beach, tracking footballs and frisbees as they arced, then zeroed in on the broken line of food trucks and felt a pang that took him by surprise. He'd barely realized at the time how well the hot dog wagon gig had suited him, how much he'd liked being part of that little world within a world within a world. Everybody was so nice. The pizza people, the taco guy, the woman who ran the Sno-Cone truck. Nobody was pushy. People helped each other out. You ran low on change, on singles, on napkins, on plates, everybody shared. Too bad the hot dog thing was crooked. Such a nice low-stress gig otherwise.

He gave a silent sigh then shifted his focus to the promenade and seawall. People were sitting on it here and there, barefoot, in their bathing suits, licking ice cream, munching tacos. Mostly they were in couples or small groups. Then Sonny's view slid past a solitary figure who was sucking a Sno-Cone from a paper cup. The Sno-Cone seemed to be either raspberry or grape and the generous mound of red-purple ice was mostly hiding the man's face. But it could be seen that his torso was lean and wiry and that he was wearing street shoes, black and pointy ones, and a shiny shirt tucked into snug black pants. Sonny panned right past at first then snapped back and stayed intent on the lone man until he lowered the Sno-Cone from his muzzle and came up for air.

Then he said, "Holy shit, it's Citarella!"

"Citarella!" echoed Bert. "Right there? Right where the hot dog used to be? What's he doin'?"

"Eatin' a Sno-Cone."

"Sno-Cone my eye. He's returnin' to the scene of the crime. Ya see? Ya see? It's just like I was sayin'. The guy who did it always comes back."

"Jeez," said Sonny, suddenly dubious, "I dunno. If he's the guy who took the hot dog, why would he come back lookin' for it?"

"Why? Ain't it obvious? He'd come back *pretendin'* to look for it, actin' all innocent, like how could he be the guy who took it if he don't even know it's missin'? It's a ruse. That much is basic. What's he doin' now? How's he look?"

"He looks like he just got syrup on his hand. He's goin' to the truck for extra napkins."

"Okay, okay, but how's he look? Guilty? Pissed off? Sneaky?"

Sonny's arms were getting heavy and his fingers were starting to cramp from twisting the tiny dials on the miniature binocs. "Guilty? Sneaky? I can't tell. Guy always looks sneaky. But wait a sec. He's throwin' away the napkins and the paper cup... Okay, now he's pacin' back and forth a little bit. He's lookin' around. He's takin' out his phone."

"Christ, I'd give a lot to know who he's callin' up right now. Be really innerestin' to know that."

An instant later Sonny's phone started ringing in his pocket. The dog barked at the sound. By reflex the big man lowered the opera glasses and made a move to answer the call.

Just as much by reflex, Bert said, "Don't do it. Don't pick up."

The phone kept ringing. The dog kept barking.

Sonny said, "But ya just said–?"

"That I'd like to know who he's callin'. And now we do. But it's not a good idea ya talk to him. Not yet. Fact is, my friend, y'ain't ready to talk. Y'ain't prepared. Look, ya talk wit' 'im, he's gonna ask a lotta questions to which you ain't got good answers. Like, for instance, where's the fuckin' hot dog?"

The phone gave one last irritating ring then stopped. The dog got a last bark in.

Bert the Shirt went on. "So, very first question and he's already got ya stumped. Not good." He gestured toward Sonny's hands. "Keep the glasses on 'im. Let's not lose 'im. S'okay, say he asks ya where the hot dog is. Maybe it's a legit question, maybe it's a bullshit question, all accordin' to whether he took the thing himself and knows exactly where it is. But either way, he's gonna ask ya, and what's your answer gonna be? It's gonna be this cockamamie story about how ya found this cat and brought it home and schmoozed a little wit' the wife, and then you went back to where the hot dog had been sittin' placidly inna moonlight just twenty minutes before and now the fuckin' thing has vanished. Due respect, Sonny, that's a cockamamie story. I happen to believe it 'cause I don't think you're the kinda guy who could make up such a thing, which I mean as a compliment to your fundamental honesty rather than a snide remark about the limits a your imagination, though I realize that maybe it didn't come out soundin' like a compliment. But anyway, not everyone is gonna believe that cockamamie story, and could ya really blame 'em if they didn't? So my suggestion or let's say strategy is that before ya tip your hand, let's see if we can find out a little more about Citarella's side a the story. In other words, my advice is that we tail 'im."

"Tail 'im?" said Sonny, his fingers trembling not from fear but from fatigue after holding the binoculars up to his eyes for the whole duration of Bert's speech. "What if he sees me? What if he recognizes me? Then I got even more explainin' to do."

"He won't recognize ya," the old man said. "I got a plan for that. Keep the glasses on 'im long as ya can. I'll grab a couple things then go downstairs and get the car. Come down when ya hear me honk three times."

8

The mangrove clearing was a very different place in the heat of afternoon. The nighttime bugs that crawled and buzzed in darkness were resting now, silent and in hiding. Spider webs drooped like double chins. Sleeping chameleons disappeared in glaring foliage. Mockingbirds and crows clattered in treetops whose supple, waxy leaves had suddenly gone dry and brittle in the sunshine. The damp ground grew parched and dusty as the sun got higher; the place went from swamp to desert nearly every day and from desert to swamp with the onset of every humid night. And the airport came alive in daytime; relentlessly alive. The outbound planes roared and bellowed. The inbound ones whined and whistled. Landing gear was extended or retracted like the claws of flying dinosaurs.

Through the heat and the racket, Pineapple and Fred were scouring the perimeter of the clearing, searching for the perfect rock to prop up their broken axle and level off the leaning hot dog. Their eyes were fixed on the ground. They used their toes to measure heft and soundness. At some point, Pineapple said, "Hey Fred, you know what I think is kind of funny?"

"No, Piney. What do you think is kind of funny?"

"Rocks."

"Rocks?"

"Well, yeah. Rocks. I mean, we see 'em every day. Lots of 'em. Thousands. Right here in the clearing. Who notices, except like, don't stub your toe? Who cares if one is round and one is square or whatever? Then all of a sudden we need a rock and now we're looking at 'em totally different, like it's a treasure hunt or something. Same rocks that've been there all along. Suddenly we're interested. I just find that kind of funny."

"I don't really see the joke," said Fred.

"I didn't say it was a joke. I just said it was kind of funny. Not everything funny has to be a joke, right?"

"What makes it funny then?"

Piney gave up trying to explain and took a different tack. "Or like, some rocks are big and some are little. Why is that? Did they start off big and little? Like, okay, this one's a boulder and that one's a pebble? Did they all break off one really gigantic rock a long time ago? I mean, was the whole world ever one big solid rock? Where'd the ocean fit if that's how it was? How'd it break? What broke it? How come some rocks are shiny and some rocks aren't? How come some are rough and some are smooth?"

"Erosion," said Fred. He didn't really know but wanted to say something smart that might wrap up the conversation.

A plane went by, outbound. They could see its flaps pulling in. Its passing made not only a noise but also a stifling pressure from the sky, as if an unseen thumb was pushing down.

"Or, like, gravel," Piney resumed when the bellow had subsided. "Gravel's funny too if you think about it. All these different kinds. All around us. Big gravel, little gravel, white gravel, black gravel. Blue. Grey. Flat. Round. But then you see these big dump trucks full of gravel and it's never all mixed up, always just one kind. How they do that, Fred?"

"Machines," Fred said authoritatively. "Sorters. They shake 'em all around and different sizes fall out different holes."

"Must be noisy."

Fred didn't bother answering.

"But even with machines," Pineapple went on, "the

pieces don't come out exactly the same. Not if you really look. I mean, there's always a few different ones mixed in. A little bigger, smaller, different color. Close but not exact. You ever really look at gravel, Fred?"

"Not like you have, Piney. But can we please find a fucking rock and get this done?"

Eventually they found a chunk of limestone that wasn't perfect but would work. Fred discovered it but it was Pineapple who dug it up with a pick and shovel that Fred had borrowed from a job site long ago. Then the tall man carried it over to the dipping corner of the hot dog and dropped it onto the ground with a seismic thud. "Heavy sucker," he allowed.

Fred, back in foreman mode, said, "Well, rest up a minute, then you can lift the wagon and I'll slide 'er under."

"Um, maybe you could help me lift the wagon," Piney suggested softly.

"What, then the thing's gonna hang in mid-air while I'm reachin' for the rock? Nah, it's gotta be division of labor. You lift, I'll get the rock in place."

Pineapple did not protest, just took a few seconds to catch his breath, shake out his hands and arms, limber up his legs. Then he braced his back against a corner of the hot dog, went into a deep squat, seized the bottom edges with his curled fingers, and lifted. Or tried to. His thigh muscles strained, his shoulder joints stretched, his face got purple, and the hot dog trembled a bit but did not come clear of the ground.

Standing by, hands on hips, Fred said encouragingly, "You're so close. Just a tiny bit more oomph. Remember to breathe. Won't hurt yourself that way. Okay. One. Two. Three..."

Piney pressed his heels into the ground, closed his eyes, and grunted. Pulse throbbed in his ears, sweat broke out at his hairline. The hot dog swayed but did not rise.

Pacing now, Fred said, "Okay, take a breather. I know what we gotta do. Smarter way to do this. We gotta shed some weight."

He went around to the high end of the wagon, climbed in, clambered across its tilting funhouse floor, and started handing things out to Pineapple through the service window. He passed along their bedrolls and canteens and tied-up bundles of extra clothes. Then he started rummaging through cabinets and cupboards and drawers, picking up momentum as he went. He handed down industrial size bottles of mustard and relish and big foaming bags of festering sauerkraut. He passed along an extra grill-top and a tray full of tongs and giant forks; an enormous stack of paper plates; a tip jar with some pennies left in it.

Trying to keep up, Piney said, "What should I do with all this stuff?"

"Just put it anywhere for now. Anywhere's fine."

He handed out a couple of frying baskets and a tub of used grease; a bag of long-defrosted, decomposing crinkle-cut potatoes; a drawer full of spoiled hot dog buns, forty-eight to the pack, and between the packs an unnoticed parcel wrapped in simple brown paper and tied up with twine.

Having tossed out nearly everything that wasn't bolted down, he stepped down from the wagon and saw how Piney had dealt with the housekeeping. Their personal possessions were neatly arrayed close to the campfire. The rest was piled in an ungainly random heap, an asymmetric alp of garbage with flashes of metal glinting here and there and oozes of wasted foodstuffs leaking from their ruined containers. "Kind of looks like crap," the tall man admitted.

"Well, we'll deal with it later," said Fred. "Maybe just set the whole mess on fire. Prob'ly easiest that way. But first things first. Let's get the wagon lifted. Should be easy now. You can do it, Piney."

9

onny kept the opera glasses trained on Citarella, tracking him as he paced a few yards up the promenade, then a few yards back, then paused to gaze for the umpteenth time at the empty place where the hot dog wagon should have been, then checked his watch, then sat down again and crossed his legs so that one pointy shoe was tapping in mid-air.

After a few minutes the big man heard three honks of a car horn. He took a final fix on his quarry and ran down to the garage, where Bert was waiting in the driver's seat of an ancient El Dorado, and Nacho, front paws braced against the window frame, was proudly posing like a misplaced hood ornament. The hulking car had once been a convertible but the springs that raised and lowered the top had rusted out during a particularly stormy summer many years before, so the roof was now permanently half-open and half-closed, like a fancy baby carriage. The tires had dark speckles where pieces of the whitewalls had flaked off. The red leather of the interior had crinkles and crosshatches like those on an elephant's trunk.

Sonny jogged around to the passenger side and got in. Bert said, "Here, put these on," and handed him a shawl, a hat, and a pair of sunglasses. The shawl was bright pink silk and was festooned with images of the Roman Coliseum, the

Leaning Tower of Pisa, and Michelangelo's statue of David; it also had a long and tickling white fringe. The hat was made of finely woven straw with a large and stylishly droopy brim accented with fabric flowers in yellow and blue. The sunglasses were rimmed with rhinestones and featured a dramatic feline upsweep at their outer edges.

Sonny looked at the accessories and said, "What the fuck, Bert?"

"Just put 'em on and slump down inna seat. Let's see how ya look."

The big man hesitated, but then, not without a certain bullfighter flair, he swirled the shawl around his shoulders and donned the hat and glasses. Appraisingly, even affectionately, Bert reached across the console and slightly adjusted the angle of the brim. "Looked better on my wife," he said, "but it'll do the job."

He edged the El Dorado out into the daylight. On the far side of A1A, Citarella was taking one last look at his watch before walking on his hard shoes toward his illegally parked Mercedes maybe fifty yards beyond the food trucks. He climbed into the car, hung a U-turn, and scudded right past the nose of Bert's old Caddy, heading toward downtown. Bert followed. Sonny hunkered low. The dog's paws ticked against the window frame.

The little convoy turned right onto Bertha Street, then made a quick left onto Atlantic Boulevard and continued past the foot of White Street Pier. At Higgs Beach, they slowed down for a moment because a topless volleyball game was underway. A couple of daytime drinkers were passed out in the gazebo. At the well-known trysting place known locally as the dick-dock, a few slender men in skimpy bathing suits were cruising. In short, everything was Key West normal. As they drove along, Sonny tested out certain variations of his outfit. He raised the shawl almost to the level of his eyes and flirtatiously dragged it back and forth like a Persian dancer. He pushed the hat back cowgirl-style but the sewn-on flowers tickled his neck. He pushed the sunglasses higher up on his flattened nose and saw the reflected rhinestones winking back at him from the windshield.

Citarella turned inland near the Flagler House Hotel, Bert the Shirt trailing a discreet two cars behind. They threaded their way through a mongrel neighborhood of manicured guesthouses interspersed with propane yards and body shops, and then, on Duval Street, the Mercedes finally parked in front of the fanciest clothing store in town, a place where everything was made by hand and came from small countries that were far away. The antique Caddy required a space-and-a-half for parking, so Bert decided the hell with it and just idled nearby between a fire hydrant and a driveway. Then they waited.

While they were waiting, Bert said, "Hey, that phone call I strongly advised you not to take. He leave a message at least?"

Sonny had forgotten all about the call. He fished his phone from a pocket and put it on speaker. Citarella's message was terse. It said, "Sonny, where the fuck are you and where the fuck's the hot dog? G'bye."

The big man in drag said, "I dunno, Bert. That just doesn't sound like a ruse to me. Sounds like he's just pissed off."

"Course it doesn't sound like a ruse," said Bert, though his conviction seemed to be waning. "What kinda crap ruse would it be if it sounded like one?"

They waited. Sonny toyed with the fringe of his shawl.

The dog jumped up and down on its master's crotch. After a couple of minutes, a woman came out onto the porch of the store. At first, not much of her could be seen because in one hand she was carrying a stack of boxes tied together with a ribbon, and in the other she was holding a few things on hangers covered over by a logo garment bag. But as she labored down the steps, maneuvering her packages for balance, Bert could see that she was a quite plump individual, maybe five foot two or three, but cantilevered up on tall sandals that didn't quite contain her chubby feet. She was big-shouldered and bosomy though didn't taper to the waist; instead, she tapered steeply and abruptly at the backside, giving her more or less the configuration of a pit bull. Her tall hair was of a magenta that did not occur in nature, and in place of eyebrows she seemed to have etched-on chevrons of dark pencil. Her lipstick was as red as an emergency and it went beyond the outline of her lips, above a chin that was soft and round.

When she'd sidestepped off the bottom stair and down to sidewalk level, Sonny, his voice hushed, a knuckle pressed reverently to his mouth through the pink silk of the shawl, said, "Oh my God, it's Cecile. Isn't she beautiful?"

Bert didn't quite know what to say to that so he didn't say anything at all. He just watched as Citarella remotely popped the trunk without stirring from the driver's seat. Cecile struggled with her purchases, stepped a bit awkwardly down from the curb, and strained to lift the boxes over the lip of the trunk. When she bent over to drape the garment bag on top, Sonny sharply drew in breath and said, "Isn't she a knockout?"

"Very striking," the old man said. Then, in deference to his passenger's devotion, he added, "Gorgeous."

She got into the car. Citarella's eyes stayed straight ahead. He drove off practically before her door was closed.

Bert followed. It wasn't much of a tail-job, maybe ten or twelve blocks in all, at a speed that never rose much over twenty. The Mercedes turned right onto Truman Avenue then threaded its way back to the Flagler House, where it pulled in under the *porte cochere* while the Caddy loitered in the shadow of a hedge. The trunk clicked open. A bellman took charge of the packages; a valet swept open the passenger door. The adored Cecile emerged one chubby foot and ankle at a time. Firmer now on her high sandals, she stepped onto the red carpet and into the hotel, Citarella catching up just as she reached the shady doorway.

In the front seat of the El Dorado, Sonny sighed. "Geez, she's amazing as ever. Just still has that special somethin' that cuts right through me. It's been, what, prob'ly a couple years since I last seen her. Feels like yesterday. Bein' with her, I think it was the happiest I ever was. Oh well."

In his reverie, he seemed to have forgotten that he was dressed in women's clothing. Remembering, he added, "Can I take these off now?"

"Sure, why not. The shawl, make sure it's folded nice. And be careful wit' the hat. I don't want it should get creased."

The big man took off his disguise and carefully placed the items in the back seat. Then he said, "Well, it was great to see 'er. Even from a distance. Can't call it a wildly successful mission, though."

"We can't?" said Bert. "I think maybe we can."

"Really? How? I mean, we didn't find out nothin'."

"Actually, I'd say we found out quite a bit."

"Like what? Guy looks for the hot dog, his wife goes shopping, he picks her up, they go to a hotel. What the hell we find out?"

Bert plucked the dog from the window frame, nestled it into his lap, and scratched its head like he was rubbing his own chin. "What we found out, my friend, is that you still got a shot wit' this woman you're so crazy about."

Sonny glanced sideways at the old man. "Come on, Bert, that's a sore spot. Don't kid me about that."

"Who's kiddin'?"

"Look, she's wit' Citarella now. They're married, for Christ's sake."

"Right, and I ain't a fan of people messin' wit' other people's spouses. But I also ain't a fan of people goin' 'round wastin' their lives not bein' happy, and it is crystal clear to me, clear as the nose on your face, that happy these two are not."

"Bert, you saw them for, like, two minutes."

"Right. And what did I see? She comes out wit' the packages. Does he help? No. Does he even get outa the car? No. He pushes a button while she wrestles wit' all that stuff. She gets in. Do they have a little smooch? No. No smooch, that's big. Do they even look at each other? No. Do they even talk? Not that I could tell. Does he ask her what she bought? Does he give a shit? Or let's look at it from her side. Does she even give him a little smile? No. Does she ask him how his day's been goin'? Sure didn't look that way to me. And why's she really buyin' all that crap inna first place? Maybe a little bit for spite? It's possible. Get mad, go shopping. Be unhappy, buy stuff. Kinda classic. Look, you know these individuals and I do not. But I was married fifty happy years, and I am telling you that there shoulda been at least a little smooch, a little smile, and that furthermore, okay, these two, they got their deal and maybe it works for them up to a certain point, but, bottom line, they don't like each other very much. It shows. It's obvious. So if you're as crazy about this woman as you seem to be, don't give up hope. That's all I'm sayin'. Ya just never know how things are gonna play."

10

Meg was doing her own special hybrid of yoga and Pilates. Specifically, she was doing boat pose, an improbable maneuver in which her legs and torso were both lifted from the mat so that her eyes were on the exact same level as her feet, her rear end being the only part of her in contact with the earth, the two halves of her body describing a shallow, graceful V, the whole elegant composition held in place by taut abs and toned hips that showed no apparent signs of strain. Her toes were pointed, her gaze was fixed on some mystic point in the middle distance, and she was so relaxed in the position that she could even speak while holding it. She was saying to her husband, "Look, honey, why keep brooding about it? Why not get it off your chest? Just talk to her. Why not?"

"Why not?" he answered. He was standing in the pool, the water up to his solar plexus, his elbows splayed out on the warm tiles of the apron. He often stood that way and watched his wife work out. Sometimes he was tempted to join in. He seldom did. It seemed like a lot of trouble. They only had one mat. Meg had sort of claimed the best spot on the deck. He wasn't used to exercise. What if he pulled something? What if he threw his back out? "Why not?" he said again. "Because she's a cat."

Meg eased out of boat pose, rolled over onto her tummy, and lifted into plank. Softly, she said, "Who *she* is, that's not the point. The point is who *you* are."

"Please let's not start with the Siddhartha crap. The point is she's a cat."

"So what? Just tell her how you feel. Why you feel that way. Let it all pour out. Why keep holding it inside?"

Peter hesitated, frowned, watched a lizard showing off its crimson throat-sac as it balanced on a hibiscus branch. Finally he looked over at Sasha, who was curled up under the lounge chair that had recently been Sonny's, her coat appearing tiger-like in the stripes thrown by the slats. Her eyes looked sleepy and uninterested. She'd been quite subdued all day. Maybe it was just the narcotic smell of the jasmine that was coming into bloom. But he couldn't help thinking that maybe she was pining, feeling a letdown at the departure of their guest; and, in the process, completely ignoring him, Peter, her benefactor and admirer.

At length he decided what the hell, what did he have to lose? He took a deep breath and let it out with a sigh. "Okay, Sasha," he began, "we need to clear the air here. I'm not trying to make you feel guilty, but you should know that it really hurt my feelings when we had a visitor and you made it very obvious that you liked him more than you like me. Why, I don't know. Because he once gave you a French fry? Because maybe he still smelled a little bit like hot dogs? Do you even like hot dogs? Anyway, you didn't sleep with me while he was here. You slept with him. Try to imagine how that made me feel. Look, you and I will be okay again. I trust that. But it's going to take a little while. You need to understand that and be extra kind and patient and gentle with me right now. Okay?"

The cat yawned.

Meg softened out of plank and lifted into cobra. "There," she said. "Don't you feel better now?"

"No, I feel like a total schmuck who just tried to explain complex and subtle emotions to a cat. I don't think she quite got all the nuance. So who should I bare my soul to next, a duck? A shrub? Maybe that would make me feel better. Maybe I'll pour my heart out to a plant. Oh, Mr. Phlox, if you only knew how much I've suffered..."

At that, Sasha for some reason roused herself from underneath the lounge. She stretched, licked her paws, smoothed her fur, then sidled over toward Peter. Arching her back and lifting her tail, she sashayed by and accepted a long stroke of his cool damp hand, then another as she pivoted and slunk past again. Then she nuzzled her forehead under his chin and purred.

"Seems to have worked," said Meg. "Just sayin'."

🌴 🌴 🌴

Fred was standing next to the pile of junk that had been tossed out of the hot dog and fiddling with a small acetylene torch that had somehow ended up in his backpack after a workday long ago but that he didn't quite remember how to use. He pointed the nozzle toward a tub of French fry grease, then opened the valve but couldn't locate the igniter. Then he found the igniter but it didn't spark. So he closed the valve and wondered how else he could light the thing. He felt in his pockets for a match. He couldn't find one. While he was searching, Pineapple said, "I don't know about this, Fred. Stuff really isn't ours to burn."

"Oh Christ, Piney, we gonna go through this again? First

it wasn't ours to take. Now it isn't ours to burn—"

"Right, 'cause so far all we did is move it from someplace to someplace else. If we burn it, then it's really gone. That's different."

"So what the hell else are we supposed to do with it? We don't burn this stuff, there's gonna be rats and there goes the neighborhood. Is that what you want? You want rats?"

"No, it's just that—"

"Look, Piney, we tried to give it back. The hot dog and everything in it. God knows we tried. In fact, if God was looking down right now, right here in this clearing, peeking right between those mangroves, you know what He'd say? He'd say, *There's those two guys that tried to give the hot dog back, but I decided that it should be theirs, including the useless, moldy crap that was in it.*"

"You think God decided that? You think God wants people to end up with stuff that isn't really theirs and then set whatever they don't want on fire?"

Fred walked it back a little. "Look, I don't know what God wants or doesn't want. I'm just tryin' to make the point that we tried our best to give it back and it didn't quite work out, so let's stop bellyachin' and make the most of it."

Piney paused a couple seconds then said softly, "You really think we tried our best?"

Fred put his hands on his hips and thrust his chin a little forward. "Course we did. We half wrecked Peter's car, for Chrissake. Course we tried our best."

"I sort of wonder if we really did. We were kind of rushed. A little lazy, maybe. Maybe we should've just drug her out like we drug her in."

"Water under the bridge, pal."

"Yeah, but ya know what I sometimes wonder about, Fred? I sometimes wonder, like, if something doesn't quite work out, and people shrug and say they tried their best, did they really try their best? Do they really believe deep down that they tried their best? And that they really, deep down, wanted it to turn out like they said they did? Or maybe, deep down, they didn't really want it to work out, they just wanted to be able to tell themselves they did. You think that ever happens, Fred?"

"So now you're sayin' we didn't try to give it back?"

"Nah, I'm not sayin' that. I'm just wondering if it ever happens that people don't exactly admit how they really want things to turn out. That's all I'm saying."

"Well, I hope you're done sayin' it, 'cause it's getting us nowhere."

He turned away from the pile of junk and went to look for a match.

Pineapple said to his back, "That French fry grease burns pretty hot, I think. Burns down restaurants sometimes. What if it sets the whole woods on fire?"

"Won't happen," Fred said over his shoulder. "Look how much open space there is."

"What about the smoke, though? What if people see it? What if the cops come? What if a fire engine shows up? Then we'd really be in trouble, Fred."

Fred turned around and flashed one of his exasperated looks, the one where his lips were pressed together and the edges of his eyes hung down like those of a played-out hound. "Piney, have you ever noticed that whenever I'm tryin' to get something done, I mean really take it by the horns and get it done, you come up with all these questions and reasons why we shouldn't do it, which really gums up the works and makes it very difficult to get anything accomplished?"

"Sorry, Fred. I just like to do things slow. So I can think 'em through. Why go faster than you can think? That's when bad things happen. Like a busted axle or something."

"Not everyone thinks as slow as you do, Piney."

"Yeah, I know."

His friend's quiet refusal to take umbrage or defend himself made Fred even more exasperated. He pointed back at the pyramid of trash. "Look," he said, "we got this big pile of shit that's gonna bring rats and stink and make the clearing a place that's really not worth living in. So I am offering a simple solution to the problem, namely burn the motherfucker up. That's too fast and easy for you? Okay. So what's your suggestion? G'ahead, I'm listening."

Pineapple took a long look at the trash heap before he answered. Then he said, "Well, we could sort the big pile into smaller piles."

"Smaller piles. Brilliant! Why didn't I think of that. S'okay, now we got a bunch of smaller crap-piles instead of one big one. Then what?"

"Then what? Well, I don't know then what. Ya see, Fred, there you go again, speeding things up, like everything has to get settled all at once. I'm saying one thing at a time. Sort 'em into smaller piles, *then* work out what to do with them."

"Ah," said Fred. "So maybe then we just sort 'em into even smaller piles, then smaller piles again."

Impervious to sarcasm, Pineapple said, "Yeah, that might be worth trying."

"And we just keep on going till they aren't piles at all, just one thin layer of garbage over the whole place and we're right back where we started."

"Nah, I think that would defeat the purpose."

Fred looked down at the ground. He slapped his palms against his thighs. He bit his lip and spat. Finally he said, "You know what, Piney? I think I'm giving up on this for now. I'm gonna take a break and let you think it through just as slow and thorough as you like. Me, I'm gonna go out and grab a couple six-packs. I'll leave ya the torch. Use it if you change your mind."

11

Bert had put the car away, and now he, Sonny, and the dog were sitting on the seawall. They told themselves they were watching out for suspicious activity in the vicinity of the food trucks, but mainly they were just looking at the beach and eating Sno-Cones. Bert was having lemon, which came close to the flavor but not the texture of the Italian ices he'd loved at Coney Island in his youth. Sonny had the one whose flavor couldn't be matched up with any fruit on earth, so they just called it blue.

It was late afternoon and the beach crowd was thinning out. Young guys crumpled one last beer can then wobbled off with their empty coolers. Women in bikinis folded up their towels and stepped into their flip-flops, their pedicures ruined by coarse sand, their skin etched with intersecting tan lines according to which bathing suit they'd worn the day before. Bert tilted his paper cup so Nacho could lap up the cold sweet syrup at the bottom; the dog came away with bright yellow droplets at the end of its muzzle. Then the old man said, "Ya know what I think our next move oughta be? I think we oughta call Citarella back."

"I thought ya said I shouldn't talk to him," Sonny pointed out. "Ya said I wasn't ready."

"Well, we know a little more now. Like where he is. Like what kinda mood he's in, namely lousy. I think it's time to feel 'im out. Maybe I can sorta help a little, do a little coachin' onna sidelines. Put 'im on speaker. Trick is, make sure ya learn more than ya teach."

Sonny looked dubious, but he threw away his Sno-Cone cup, sat down on the wall again, cleared his throat, and made the call.

Citarella picked up on the second ring. He didn't say hello. He said, "Sonny, where the fuck you been?"

"Around," the big man said. "Here and there."

Bert nodded approvingly at the laconic reply.

"And where's the fuckin' hot dog?"

"Ya know, I was just gonna ask you that."

"You telling me you don't where it is?" said Citarella, shouting over television noise on his end of the line. Then he said, "Hang on a minute." Then he yelled out, "Will you turn that fucking TV down? I'm on an important call."

A woman's voice, muffled by distance but not soft, said "Bigshot. It's so important, go talk onna balcony."

Sonny covered his phone with his hand. To Bert, he said, "Ah, that Cecile. She don't let no one push her around."

Citarella got back to business. "So lemme get this straight. You're tellin' me you don't know where the hot dog is?"

Sonny said, "Well, I kinda been out lookin' for it."

"But you don't where it is?"

"Frankie, if I knew where it was, why would I be lookin'?"

Bert offered a thumbs-up for this bit of repartee.

Citarella sounded less impressed. "Don't get cute with

me, Sonny. It doesn't suit you." Then he shouted out, "I said turn the fucking television down."

"Screw you," said Cecile. "It's just at the part where she decides which bachelor she wants. Hope to Christ she picks better than I did."

This rated another thumbs-up from Bert.

Citarella now sounded in equal parts furious and dazed. "You lost the fuckin' hot dog. I cannot believe you lost the fuckin' hot dog. How much of a loser can a person be? This whole complicated set-up, you got one tiny little piece of it— take care of the hot dog wagon. And you fuck it up. How dumb can you be?"

Sonny reddened and his fingers tightened on the phone. He didn't care that much if Citarella called him names, but he didn't like being run down in front of Cecile. Bert gestured that he should stay calm and turn the other cheek. The big man kept quiet.

"And now we're both in deep shit 'cause of you," Citarella went on. "Very deep. I got Charlie Ponte up my ass. Ponte's got Fat Lou up his. And even Lou, he's gonna have a big problem wit' Livingstone."

"Livingstone?" Bert mouthed.

Sonny shrugged.

"And why?" Citarella rolled on. "'Cause my good friend Sonny, who I trusted and vouched for, can't even keep track of a goddamn hot dog wagon. And tomorrow I gotta sit down wit' these hotshots and tell them that the whole thing's all screwed up 'cause the guy I trusted couldn't do the job."

At the mention of a sit-down, Bert leaned in very close to Sonny's phone, pushed out his flubbery lips, pulled in a deep breath, and tried his best to imitate the sound of a Harley while also signaling for time out.

"Hang on," said Sonny, "I got a couple motorcycles goin' by."

He wiped a few flecks of spit from his face and covered up the phone.

Bert said, "We gotta be at that meeting."

"We?"

"Push a little now. Now's the time to push."

Back on the line, Sonny said, "So Frankie, that sit-down. I think I oughta be there."

Citarella seemed to find this amusing. "You? There? That's rich. You don't seem to grasp that this is way above your level. You ain't gonna be there, pal, on accounta you ain't invited."

Bert urged him to press on.

"Look, if I'm gettin' blamed here, I should at least be able to tell my side."

"Your side? You ain't got a side. Your side is you lost the fuckin' hot dog wit' a shipment in it. That's the long and short of it."

A fresh cascade of television noise poured from the phone, apparently the racket of amped-up applause at the end of a show. Citarella yelled out, "*Now* can you turn it down?"

"Yeah, fine, whatever," Cecile hollered back. "She picked the wrong guy anyway. Figures."

To Sonny, Citarella said, "Look, I got one piece of advice for you. Find the wagon by noon tomorrow. Don't make me sit down wit' these guys and tell 'em you blew it. It comes to that, I'd feel a little bad for ya. Old friends and all. Good luck."

12

It was a long, hot walk to Gator Liquors—out of the mangroves, up around the north end of Key West, then across the abutment of the Cow Key Bridge, then down again along Roosevelt Boulevard, past ranks of pastel, Gulf-side condos that didn't used to be there, past the chain motels and fast-food joints that had gradually displaced the funky one-offs that had gotten by for decades on so-called local charm in spite of their mildewed sheets, greasy fritters, and deranged night managers—and by the time Fred reached the fading strip mall that used to be anchored by a Sears, he was ready to sit down at his favorite dive bar, Stick and Stein, and to enjoy some air-conditioning before proceeding to the package goods shop conveniently located right next door. He was also ready for some extra time away from Pineapple, with his endless questions and loony observations. Not that he didn't love the guy. And of course he knew that Piney would be completely helpless without him. That this would be equally true vice-versa never really occurred to Fred.

In any case, he counted up the money in his pocket and decided he could have a draft or two, since, during off-hours on weekdays, they only cost a buck apiece. It was worth it just to get off his feet and feel the tingle of the A/C on the back of his neck.

He went into the bar. It was dim. It was cool. It was heavenly. He ordered a beer. A couple of guys with whom he occasionally did day-labor came in and they got to talking. He ordered a refill. A pool game got started on the ancient table with its dead rails and scabby bald spots on the felt. Two beers became four. The guy who lost the pool game snapped a cue across his knees and added it to the rack of broken sticks. Then he bought a round for everybody and all was instantly forgiven.

By the time Fred got back to the clearing, balanced by a six-pack held in either hand, the temperature had dropped by ten degrees, the sun was almost down, and where the pyramid of piled trash had stood, there was nothing but a smoldering patch of ashes, the occasional ember still glowing orange in the softening light, a live cinder now and then sailing away on an updraft. He put the beer in the cooler and said, "Jesus, Piney, how'd you do all that?"

"Slowly," said the tall man. "Little by little."

"I figured that. But little by little how?"

"Well, the metal stuff, I put it back inside the hot dog. Why not? It's still good. Didn't want to see it go to waste. Paper plates, napkins, I kept as much as we might use. The rest of the stuff I burned in little batches. Spoiled food mostly. The taters, the rolls, the sauerkraut. Whatever was in there and went bad. I used the French fry grease to keep it burning, a little at a time so it wouldn't smoke too much. Worked good. Then I carted some containers to the dumpster by the airport, and that was that. Wasn't too bad if you take it step by step."

Fred felt vaguely guilty that he hadn't been there to help, but it was a feeling he'd dealt with many times before and he seemed to get over it quickly. "Well, ya did good, Piney. I gotta say it. Ya did really good."

Pineapple gave a modest shrug and glanced around the

clearing. "Makes it feel more like a real home, don'tcha think, Fred? When you do some work around a place, I mean. I think about that sometimes. Like, with people who own stuff, who live in regular houses. They fix things up. They paint the place. They mow the lawn. Probably it's a real pain in the neck sometimes, but people do it. Why do you think that is, Fred?"

"How 'bout 'cause they have to?"

"Well, that's the part I wonder about. Do they have to? Not really. They could let the place go. Some people do. Most people don't. How come?"

"Well, for one thing, they'd get all kinds of shit from the neighbors."

"I guess. But let's leave the neighbors on the side for now. Or let's pretend there aren't any neighbors. I think most people would still keep their place fixed up. Maybe just 'cause it reminds them that they own it, that it's really theirs. I guess it makes them feel good, proud maybe, like they earned the place."

"Earned it?" Fred harrumphed. "Probably they just went out and bought it."

"Right, but this is what I'm saying. There's buying and there's earning. You think they're exactly the same thing, Fred? I think maybe they aren't. Especially if you don't have any money. Anyway, that's kind of how I feel now. Like we've earned the place, I mean. Like we fixed things up, made 'em better, so it's okay to live here now. That feels good. I like the way it feels. You ready for some dinner?"

"Cholly? It's Bert d'Ambrosia callin'.'"

"Bert d'Ambrosia? Bert the Shirt? You old fossil, you uncle of a dinosaur. So you're still breathin'?"

"Last I checked. And how's the state a your health, if I may so inquire?"

"Lousy. Blood pressure's through the roof. Cholesterol's off the charts. Passed a stone last week. So what the hell ya want from me this time?"

"Want from ya?" said Bert in an affronted tone, while petting his dog and giving his houseguest Sonny a wink. They were sipping espresso laced with anisette from chipped cups at the table with the boomerang pattern. "Jesus, what's the world comin' to when a guy can't pick up the phone and call an old friend wit'out it bein' assumed or presumed or otherwise taken for granted in what is, let's face it, a rather skeptical or even cynical way that he must be callin' t'ask for somethin'?"

"Cut the bullshit, Bert. What ya want?"

"Well, okay Cholly, since y'insist on puttin' it in such a cut-and-dried or matter a fact or even transactional, I think the word is, sorta way, what I want is the pleasure of takin' ya to lunch tomorrow. Someplace nice, up by you. Stone crab, lobster, anything ya like. On me. Just to catch up a little bit."

Charlie Ponte looked out through his Miami penthouse window, down at the boats making crisscross wakes in Biscayne Bay. He couldn't deny that he felt a certain bond with Bert, maybe even a grudging affection, based mainly on a shared knack for survival in what was often a brutal business. Still, he gave the lunch invitation about a two percent chance of being on the level. Then again, wouldn't it be nice to imagine that someone might invite him out to lunch without a quid pro quo involved? Wouldn't it be nice if *anyone* took *anyone* to lunch without wanting something back? Not letting down his guard, but not without a slight hint of rue either, he said, "It's a nice thought, thanks, but I'm busy tomorrow."

"Ah, too bad," the old man said, rubbing the dog's head like he was stroking his own chin. "But ya know, I had a funny feelin' ya might be tied up tomorrow. 'Specially at lunchtime. I just had a feelin' ya might be busy then."

Ponte got over his brief spasm of wistfulness and became his usual suspicious self again. "Where we goin' wit' this, Bert?"

The old man silently clinked his espresso cup against Sonny's. "Well, I just thought, noon tomorrow, ya might, fr'instance, be in a meetin' wit' a guy named Citarella and maybe a representative of Fat Lou, or who knows, maybe even Lou himself, pertainin' to a certain situation here in Key West involvin' a delayed or perhaps, God forbid, even botched pickup of, uh, well, let's just say a botched pickup. Anyway, what I'm comin' round to is that I thought you mighta had a previous engagement, aka a sitdown."

"How the hell you know about that?"

"Well, you know me, Cholly. I hang around. I talk to people. I hear stuff. Like if there's gonna be a sitdown. Like if a guy named Livingstone might be involved."

"Livingstone? Nobody knows about Livingstone."

"On that point I must beg to differ. A certain select few do. Includin' me. And by the way, since we're onna subject, it's only fair t'inform you, or clue you in, I guess you could say, that I also know a thing or two of which even you yourself might not be, whaddyacallit, cognizant, or let's just say ya wouldn't know about it, and that it might possibly be in your interest if I was to share these informations at tomorrow's sitdown."

"At the sitdown? Bert, are you crazy? Don't try to stick your nose in this. It has nothing to do with you."

"Well, that depends on how ya look at it, Cholly. Strictly speakin', I guess, yeah, it's none a my business. But say, fr'instance, if it so happened that there was a certain vending wagon that was kinda central to the subject under discussion, and if said vending wagon was right across the street from where I live and I saw it every single fuckin' day, and furthermore if this vending wagon was inna shape of a giant hot dog and run by a guy who happens to be a friend a mine, well, now we're gettin' into a grey area where the case could be made that maybe it is my business and, furthermore, that I might even have somethin' useful to contribute."

Ponte had time for three sips of Mylanta while Bert was talking. When it was finally his turn to speak, he said, "Fuck you know about the hot dog and the loser who runs it?"

"Cholly, I'd rather not go into it onna phone right now wit'out the other innerested parties present. I mean, isn't this exactly the reason we have sitdowns? To discuss exactly these sortsa complicated matters where one guy says somethin' and the other guy says somethin' else, and we try to get things settled, and wit'out gettin' all highfalutin' about it, we try to make it come out right so justice is done and nobody gets steamrolled or otherwise fucked innee ass on accounta he wasn't invited to the meetin' and didn't get to have his say. So, bottom line, I'm suggestin' we continue the conversation tomorrow at the sitdown where I and my friend, who happens to be good people, can put our cards onna table along wit' everybody else, and the table's gonna be level, although I guess it's usually the playin' field that people say oughta be level, but anyway, it comes down to the same thing. So whaddya say, Cholly? We invited?"

13

That night the cat wandered off again.

It was around three a.m. when Peter woke up for a pee and noticed that her small weight had been subtracted from the bed, her concentrated warmth missing from the little canyon between his feet. In a drowsy state between drugged sleep and reluctant waking, he suddenly felt the onset of a disturbing, even panic-inducing, sense of déjà vu. The situation, in every minute detail, was so eerily familiar: the wrinkles in the sheet where the cat had been; his wife's cheek pressed at a certain angle against her pillow as she serenely slumbered on; the thin cotton curtain swaying in its same easy but obsessive rhythm in the moonlight and the humid breeze. Hadn't he lived this exact moment before? Recently? Just two nights ago? Was he for some unknowable reason destined to live it again and again? Was this fated to be his new routine, his personal version of normal: Wake up in the middle of the night, realize that the cat is missing, go searching like some half-mad pilgrim; end up getting hauled off in a hot dog, knocked unconscious, then shanghaied, by a crazy mix of circumstance, guilt, compassion, cowardice, and just plain being who he was, into this tangled matrix of other people's problems, among which was being homeless and/or in big trouble with the Mob? Would this be his life from now on? The whole sequence, again and again, starting with the absent cat?

Would it happen over and over until he perished from exhaustion?

He took a few deep breaths, as his wife always counseled, and half a Xanax just in case the non-pharmaceutical approach came up short.

He padded off to the bathroom and started softly calling to the cat. That got him nowhere. Then he had a hopeful though ambivalent hunch as to where she might be. He went into the guest bedroom. It would have given him a pang to find Sasha curled up in the bed where she'd so recently slept with Sonny, but at least he would have found her. Except she wasn't there.

He went downstairs in his pajamas and out to the backyard. The moon was reflected in the swimming pool. The air smelled of jasmine and damp boards. There was no cat. Somehow he'd known there'd be no cat, but still, it was disheartening. His shoulders slumped. He sighed. He went into the kitchen, grabbed his car key, and headed to the driveway.

He'd forgotten for the moment how shitty his car looked with the bumper torn off, the paint job all scratched up as though raked by malevolent claws, the windshield smeared with mangrove sap and the filth that clung to it. He'd never felt an emotional response to his car before, but just then he saw it as an object worthy of pity but also some instinctual disgust. If he saw a stranger driving a car like that, he'd guess that the poor bastard lived a chaotic, reckless, squalid life full of bad decisions and cigarette butts and encounters with the repo man.

He got in, started the engine, and began weaving through the maze of streets around the cemetery, windows rolled down, calling, "Sasha...Sasha," in a singsong and almost pleading tone of voice. After he'd combed the immediate neighborhood, he headed to the beach, crawling up the A1A until he'd almost reached the food trucks, at which point he saw, in silhouette, a lone, large figure sitting on the seawall, legs dangling over the sand; also in silhouette, he could see the distinctive, triangular shapes of a pair of cat's ears protruding from the seated figure's lap. He slammed on the brakes and parked just behind the pizza truck.

"Sonny!" he called, as he spun out of the squalid car. "You have my cat!"

"Oh, hey Peter," the big man said casually. "Yeah, she just came by a coupla minutes ago."

"And you just happened to be sitting here."

"Yeah. Couldn't sleep. Big day tomorrow. Lot on my mind." He looked Peter up and down. "Nice pajamas."

"Thank you. I seem to be wearing them to the beach quite often lately."

Sonny stroked the cat from ears to tail. "Me, I can't wear pajamas. They bunch up here and there, make me twitchy. I gotta sleep wit' nothin' on."

"I really didn't need to know that."

"Yeah, well, whatever. Just makin' conversation. Anyway, right when you pulled up, I was tryin' to decide if I should bring the cat to your place or wait till morning. Didn't want to wake you and the missus again if I could help it."

"Very considerate. But since I'm awake now anyway, I'll bring her home. Thanks."

He reached for the cat in Sonny's lap. At the last instant, the cat sprang away, landed on the promenade, and meowed loudly.

Peter, his feelings wounded, said, "Jeez, she never does that. Jumps away when I reach for her. Never. That just doesn't happen."

"She's a funny cat, all right."

"I just don't know what's going on. It's like she's mad at me all of a sudden. What the hell did I do? I have no idea."

"Ah, don't take it personal. Cats are cats. Gotta roll wit' it."

"Easy for you to say. You, she's crazy about." Then, in a purring sort of voice, he said, "Sasha. Come here, Sasha."

The cat meowed again, then took a couple steps farther away, northbound, toward the airport, toward where the road bent left and shortly afterward gave access to a narrow path that led on to a certain secret clearing in the mangroves. Then she looked back across her shoulder.

"Come on, pretty kitty. Time to go home."

She took two more steps, looked back again, and seemed to wag her chin.

"Weird," said Sonny. "It's almost like she's tryin' to tell us somethin'."

That made Peter very nervous. "Nah, she's just being difficult." He stepped stealthily toward her. She kept her distance.

"Sure looks like she's tryin' to."

"Come on, what could she possibly have to tell us? I mean, it's not like she's a dog."

"Dog? Who said anything about a dog?"

Nervous, guilty, Peter said, "Did I mention dog? I just

meant, you know, about smelling something, picking up a scent."

"Ah, like following a trail," said Sonny. "That's inneresting. I hadn't thought of that."

"Well, doesn't matter. It's what dogs do. Cats don't do it."

Sasha, meanwhile, had wandered over to the curb where the hot dog wagon used to be. She daintily stepped down onto the edge of the roadway and sniffed at it with interest.

"Wonder what she's smellin'."

"Urine probably. That's mostly what cats smell. Urine."

"You know best, I guess. She used to really like the smella hot dogs, though. Or maybe it was the fries. Who could tell which smell she liked? But she definitely liked somethin'. I mean, after that one French fry I gave her, she came back to the wagon all the time. Never quite knew how she found it. Never really thought about it till now. Wonder if she still remembers. Wonder if she's gettin' a whiffa hot dogs now."

"Um, I really doubt it. Short memory, this cat."

At that, she glanced back once again, sneezed, groomed her whiskers, and edged a few steps farther on, her flank against the curb.

"Maybe we should follow 'er," said Sonny.

"Nah, I don't think that's a good idea."

"Ain't ya curious? Just curious, I mean? Me, I'm kinda curious. Nice to try to figure what an animal is thinkin'."

"Well, yeah," said Peter, "but, well, look, I'm standing here in my pajamas, it's the middle of the night–"

"Maybe just a little ways. See where she's headed. I'll go.

I find it kinda fascinatin'."

The big man swung his legs down from the seawall. The cat meowed, lifted its tail, and continued on. Sonny followed. Peter, his throat constricted with misgivings, felt he had no choice but to tag along as the odd procession inched northward in the moonlight. He badly wished he'd brought along the second half of his pill.

14

"They call this fresh-squeezed?" said Cecile, bundled in her hotel bathrobe at the room-service breakfast table that had been rolled onto the balcony of their room at the Flagler House. She hadn't been awake long enough to fix her hair. It was flat on the side where she slept and flyaway on the other, as if she was sitting in a windstorm, though the morning air was heavy and still. "My eye it's fresh-squeezed. Who do they think they're kidding? Like people can't tell it's straight from a carton?"

Her husband was already showered and dressed in his snug pants and shiny shirt and pointy shoes. He sat across from her but looked out absently toward the ocean as he ate toast and drank coffee.

"Melon's hard as a rock," she said.

He looked down at his watch.

She ate some unripe melon. While chewing it, she fingered the bloom in the obligatory bud vase next to the sad little basket of re-warmed baked goods. "Already wilting," she said. "What's it, 8 a.m.? Flowers'll be dead as doornails by noon."

Citarella poured himself more coffee.

"I'll take a warm-up, too," said his wife. "Thanks for asking."

He spilled some into her cup then looked at his watch again. "We need to get a move on."

She reached into the basket for a miniature Danish with a smear of yellowish cheese in the center. "I happen to be enjoying my breakfast at the moment. Do you mind?"

"I need to be somewhere, Cecile."

"And I like it here on the balcony. It's beautiful. It's peaceful. Why do we always have to be in such a hurry?"

"We don't always have to be in such a hurry. Right now we're in a hurry so I have time to drop you home and get to a meeting. An important meeting."

"Important meeting. With you, it's always an important meeting. You need to do something, it's important. I need to do something, it's not important. We go where you wanna go. We leave when you wanna leave–"

He stood up from the table and threw his napkin down. "Don't start with this shit now, Cecile. Please. I'm a little wound up and you're really gettin' on my nerves."

"Oh, I am? Like you're not gettin' on mine? Like it's a one-way street who's gettin' on whose nerves? It's not a one-way street. It's a two-way street. And I'll tell ya what gets on my nerves, Frankie. What gets on my nerves is I don't like the way you treat me lately. Mostly you ignore me. 'Cept when you're bossin' me around. Would it kill ya to be a little nicer? You pour yourself more coffee. Would it kill ya to say, *Need a refill, honey?* Would it kill ya to say *How's the Danish?*"

"Look, Cecile, I don't have time for this."

"I mean, like, here we are, nice hotel. Bathrobes. Bud vase. Ocean view. Could be very nice. Could be romantic, right? Does it dawn on you for half a second to be romantic?

Have some candles, maybe? Some flowers, some chocolates. Make a little fuss. Wash my back for me maybe. Gaze into each other's eyes. Or maybe just talk to each other for a change. Talkin' to each other, that'd be a start."

"We are talkin'," Citarella said. "Or you're talkin', at least. Complaining mostly. And I'm a little sicka hearin' it right now. So will you please finish up your goddamn breakfast and throw some clothes on so we can get outa here and I can drop ya home?"

"Drop me home. Drop me home. Like, what, droppin' off the groceries? The dry cleaning? Well, ya know what? I don't wanna be dropped home and I don't wanna rush. I like it where I am. I wanna take my time, enjoy the view, have a leisurely breakfast, relax."

"You're makin' me late, Cecile. We gotta go."

"No, Frankie. We don't gotta go. You gotta go. Me, I'm gonna stay. Keep the room another day or two. Have a look around. Not be in such a freakin' hurry. Good luck at your meeting."

⚓ ⚓ ⚓

Bert and Nacho and Sonny had already been on the road a while. They needed a head-start, considering how slowly the old man drove, even though he was dressed like a throwback race car driver in a white scarf, kid gloves, and a tattersall snap-brim cap. The dog had a tiny cap and scarf to match, in addition to racing goggles that kept the grit out of its bulging eyes when it leaned beyond the window frame. Wind whistled softly through the opening in the paralyzed convertible roof as mile after mile of the Florida Keys drifted by in slow motion, pale green water on the Gulf side, aquamarine studded with maroon coral heads at the verge of the Atlantic. Where there was land, there were dusty trailer parks and bars with tiki roofs and low motels dwarfed by their looming Deco signs. Traffic stacked up behind the ancient El Dorado, horns honking, drivers occasionally giving Bert the finger when they finally got a chance to pass. He smiled and waved at them in a friendly manner then went back to having both hands on the wheel.

The silver pushbuttons on the radio had stopped moving the pointer many years before, and anyway, the antenna had long ago snapped off, leaving only a rusty chrome ring where it used to be attached. Sonny was fidgety and really could have used some music. In its absence, he tapped his foot against the floor and settled for sudden bursts of largely disconnected conversation.

When they were just south of Big Pine, he suddenly said, "Peter and his cat were actin' really strange last night."

"Excuse me?"

"Peter. Ya know. The worried guy."

Bert just nodded.

"Him and his cat were actin' very strange."

"You were wit' them last night? Last I knew, you were sleepin' onna couch."

"Well, not sleepin', was the problem. Too wound up. Anyway, so I go down to the beach, I'm sittin' onna seawall by the food trucks, and along comes the cat. Who knows why? Maybe just coincidence. Maybe the cat has some crazy sixth sense and knows I'm gonna be there. Who knows? Anyway, I'm a little lonely and I'm glad to see 'er. So I make this little sound she likes, kind of a soft click wit' my tongue, and she jumps into my lap. Coupla minutes later, Peter comes along in his pj's."

"In his pj's?"

"Well, yeah, it's the middle of the night."

"But no robe or nothin'?"

"Nah, just pj's."

"Me, I go out to walk the dog, pick up a newspaper, whatever, I got the decency to put a robe on."

"Well, wit' Peter it's just pj's, what can I say? He takes a lotta sleepin' pills, I think. Who knows if he's even sure when he's awake or he's asleep? But anyway, where I was goin' wit' this—"

"Nice pj's at least? Matching?"

"Yeah. Nice. I mean, look, I'm no expert, but yeah, they seemed like nice pajamas. The button-down kind. Like in old movies where they can't make it look like anybody sleeps naked. Baby blue. But can we please move on from the pajamas? Where I was goin' wit' this is that we chat a little bit, then he goes to take the cat, and the cat jumps away from him, which hurts his feelings, and he comes right out and says so, and I'll tell ya the truth, I feel his pain, I really do, 'cause there's this cat he's so devoted to, so crazy about, and then she goes off sittin' in somebody else's lap and suddenly it's like he don't exist. And I'm thinkin' it's a lot like me and Cecile. I mean, okay, not a perfect comparison, cats and people, but the way it hurts, it's gotta be similar, let's face it. So I feel bad for the guy, but what can I do? The cat likes me."

They stopped for a red light. Beyond it, the speed limit dropped in deference to strip malls and however many Key deer had not already been run over. Bert drove even slower. Glancing over at Sonny, he said, "Okay, so the cat's fickle and the guy wears pajamas. What's the strange part?"

"Well, I'm gettin' to it," the big man said. "So the cat jumps away. Peter goes to pick her up. She moves a little farther. Then she starts sniffin' at the ground, right where the hot dog used to be. Then she looks back at us. She looks at Peter. She looks at me. Those green eyes keep shuttlin' back and forth. She goes a few steps up the curb. I'm wonderin' if she's tryin' to tell us somethin'. I mention this to Peter. He starts gettin' nervous."

"He's always nervous," Bert put in.

"Okay, fair enough. But now's he's gettin' more nervous. Then, outa the blue, he says, *Well, it's not like she's a dog.* Which was weird, 'cause up to that second, it never even occurred to me that, yeah, she was kinda actin' like a dog. Findin' things by smell, I mean. How'd she find me sittin' onna seawall? How'd she find the empty place where the hot dog used to be? Plus by then she starts sorta gliding her way along the curb, sniffin' as she goes, and I start thinkin', well, if she could sniff her way to where the hot dog used to be, maybe she could sniff her way to where it is now. I mean, it's a million to one shot, but what the hell else we got to go on? And besides, I'm partly just plain curious. So I say let's follow 'er. Peter tries to talk me out of it, but I do it anyway, so he comes along.

"And the cat keeps movin' along the curb, sniffin', lookin' back, gettin' closer toward the airport. Peter's gettin' more nervous alla time, don't ask me why, but I mean, ya could see it. He's takin' bigger steps, he's leanin' forward, his veins are poppin' out. When the cat isn't lookin' back, he's tryin' to get closer, like sneakin' up on her. I mean, it's like he's stalkin' his own pet cat. Weird, right? Anyway, long story short, we're almost even wit' the airport, he takes a flyin' leap and tackles 'er."

"Tackles 'er?" said Bert. "He tackles his own cat?"

"That's sure how it looked to me. I mean, okay, maybe he just made a grab for her and tripped, who's to say? He's not the most athletic kinda guy, but anyway, bottom line, it looked like a tackle and he ends up rollin' onna ground wit' the cat in his arms. The cat's screamin' and clawin' at his chest. He's all of a sudden got these ragged holes in the knees of his nice pajamas from where he went down. Rough pavement up there. So he rolls around till he manages to stand up, then he says somethin' like, *Okay, enough already. It's ridiculous. Two grown men. How long we gonna watch a cat smell urine?*"

Bert said, "Urine? What's urine got to do wit' it?"

"That's what Peter says she was sniffin'. All along. From the start. Urine. Ya know, how they mark territory, how they know who's been around."

Bert took one hand off the wheel to scratch Nacho's head through the fabric of the tattersall cap. "Sorry, I'm a little bit confused right now. You're followin' the cat. You think the cat's smellin' hot dogs. Peter thinks the cat's smellin' cat pee. So what the hell's the cat smellin'?"

"Well, that's the thing," said Sonny. "Who knows? Anyway, bottom line, we're up by the airport, Peter says, *That's it, we're goin' home.* And he starts walkin' back. So I go wit' 'im. What else can I do? It's his cat."

He broke off with a shrug and drummed a few beats on the dashboard.

Bert said, "So that's it? That's the enda the story? We don't know where the cat was goin'?"

"Nope."

"Kinda unsatisfyin'."

"What can I say? I'm just tellin' ya what happened. But okay, there's one other thing I thought was kinda strange. So I'm walkin' him back to his car and when we get there I see it's all fucked up. Bumper missin'. Paint all scratched. And I'm tryin' to remember if that's the way it was the first time I saw it. I mean, I stayed at their place two nights. The car was inna driveway. First day I saw it, I think it was fine. I mean, I think I woulda noticed if it was all messed up. So I'm lookin' at the guy, and I'm thinkin', man, he's havin' a rough week. He's onnee outs wit' his cat. His pj's are wrecked and his knee is bleedin'. Plus now his car is all fucked up. So I feel bad for him. So, very sympathetic like, I say, *Dude, what happened to your car?* And this seems to make 'im nervous all over again. So he kinda waves over toward the beat-up thing like everything's hunky-dory wit' it, like it's fresh outa the showroom, and says, *Happened? Um, well...uh, nothing. Nothing happened.* And he throws the cat in the car and drives away. And that was that."

Bert kept petting the dog with one hand and making tiny steering adjustments with the other. "So lemme make sure I have this right," he said. "The cat was smellin' somethin' but ya don't know what. It was goin' someplace but ya don't know where. The car got dinged up but ya don't know when or how. Anythin' else ya don't know but would like to tell me all about?"

"Nah," said Sonny. "That pretty well sums it up."

Bert said, "Okay, very edifyin'," and continued driving at a stately pace toward the sitdown in Miami.

"Fred," said Pineapple, "ya know what I sometimes wonder about?"

They were sitting on rocks around the campfire in the clearing, drinking coffee from tin mugs and eating the last of their stash of bacon from Fred's most recent stint of day-work. The embers from Piney's bonfire had long been cool; most of the ash had blown away, leaving just a vague charred circle of coral nubs and gravel on the ground. At their backs, the hot dog wagon where they'd slept was standing pretty close to level, it's service window and back door wide open to let the morning breeze blow through.

"No, Piney, what do you sometimes wonder about?"

"I sometimes wonder, well, if we lived in a world that was a little different from the one we're living in—not too much different, more alike than different, really—but say if it never got cold, and never rained, and there were no hurricanes and no mosquitoes and no bad people who might sneak along and steal your stuff, would people still feel like they had to live in houses?"

Fred washed down some bacon with a swig of coffee. "What's the difference, Piney? There's never gonna be a world like that."

"Yeah, I know. But let's leave that on the side for now. What if there was? Would people still want houses so, like, they could paint theirs blue if the next guy's house was yellow? Or so they could have a door that people had to knock on and they could say come in or don't come in, depending on whether they liked the person who was knocking? But then again, what if they didn't really know the person who was knocking? Do they let him in or leave him standing outside?"

"Ya leave 'im standing," Fred put in. "Better safe than

sorry."

"Well, I guess that's what the door is for. But if you don't know the person yet, and if you don't let him in, how are you ever gonna know whether you like him or not? No door, at least you could meet the guy and decide."

"Yeah, and if he's a jerk or a pervert," said Fred, "then you're stuck with him."

"Not if you weren't in a house. If you weren't in a house, you could just go someplace else. Or what if you're in your house and the roof caved in and you got trapped? House wouldn't seem like such a hot idea if the roof caved in."

"You just said there wouldn't be hurricanes."

"Right. No hurricanes. But there's still gravity, so roofs are gonna cave in now and then. So what if you're trapped with your walls on top of you and your furniture all busted up and no one can get through all that stuff to help you? Good idea to have a house if that happens? Or, like, take cooking smells."

"Cooking smells? How'd we get to cooking smells?"

"I'm just thinking about the good points and bad points of living in a house. 'Cause everyone just sees the good parts, so they think it's something everyone just automatically would want, and if it isn't what you want, there must be something wrong with you. But say you're cooking up some fish. You do that in a house, it stinks for days. You do it outside, the fish tastes good and you're done. So there's plusses and minuses. That's all I'm saying. Not automatic that a house is better. Good if it's raining, true. Good if it's buggy, true. But all in all, if the sun is out and it's nice and warm, I'd rather be outside. Who wouldn't?"

15

Nacho snarled as Bert was being patted down in the foyer of Charlie Ponte's penthouse. "Go easy," the old man advised, "or this dog'll rip ya to shreds."

Unimpressed, unsmiling, the flunkey worked his rough hands into Bert's groin and armpits, then did the same with Sonny. Then they were ushered into the dining room where three men were sitting at a long mahogany table, each with two bodyguards stationed behind.

One of the seated men was Ponte himself—pudgy, thick-necked, bald on top, with the affronted expression of a man whose digestion has betrayed him. Then there was the mountainous Fat Lou, who'd picked up a double order of stone crab claws on the drive down from the airport and was eating them straight out of their cardboard box, dipping them in a plastic container of mustard sauce and not offering any to anybody else. The third man was all sour elegance— tall, lean, dressed in off-white linen, his long face largely hidden by a Panama hat crimped and molded perfectly and a pair of wraparound shades whose mirrored lenses shot back stretched and melting images of the room around him.

The greetings were terse. Fat Lou grunted his hellos with his mouth full. The elegant man, introduced only as Livingstone, didn't deign to speak just then but only raised two fingers to the brim of his hat and pulled it a millimeter farther down across his eyes. Bert slowly and creakily sat down and got the chihuahua settled in his lap. Sonny hesitated. He hadn't been to many sitdowns, and during those rare ones he'd attended he'd never been offered a chair but always stood up with the underlings. Bert now pulled one back for him and he eased down onto the edge of it.

Then there was a moment that was silent except for Fat Lou's chewing. The moment stretched on until Livingstone tugged up a shirt cuff and looked down at his Rolex.

To no one in particular, Ponte said, "Where the fuck is Citarella?" Then, to Bert, he added, "He didn't drive up with you?"

Bert said, "I think its kinda obvious he didn't. I don't even know the man."

Livingstone shook his head. "So typical of your people," he said to Lou and Ponte. It was tough to place his accent. It wasn't British, though it was close. Mainly it was snooty. "Undisciplined. Disorganized. Not punctual."

The bald part of Ponte's head flushed purple but he kept quiet. Fat Lou wiped his mouth and said, "Citarella's always been solid."

By way of reply, Livingstone just smirked and looked down at his watch again.

Some seconds later, the tardy man, jumpy and frazzled, was led into the room. There were places on his shiny shirt that were dark with sweat; his hair was slicked down in damp bundles. Against the disapproving glares that were aimed at him from all around the table, he tried his best to smile, to explain, to show what a regular guy he was and get people on his side.

"Sorry I'm late, gentlemen," he said. "My pain innee ass

wife picks today of all days to pick a fight with me. Just grabs on and won't let go. Tellin' me I ain't nice enough to her. Not romantic. Can you believe that shit? I got a meetin' to get to, she's bustin' my balls about flowers and chocolate. Makes me late then won't leave the hotel. Decides she's gonna stay. Just like that. Woman's a real bitch sometimes."

"Ya don't talk about Cecile that way," Sonny blurted out. He hadn't known he was about to speak. That hadn't been the plan. He wasn't going to speak till spoken to, and, even then, he'd been counseled to say as little as possible. But he just couldn't let this pass.

Citarella propped his hands on his hips. "Oh, I don't? Well, I just did."

"It ain't right, Frankie. It's disrespectful."

The wiry man seemed to find this amusing or at least pretended to in front of the others. "Disrespectful? Not right? And who the fuck are you, some hot dog-selling Sir Galahad? Who by the way she dumped the second something better came along? She's my wife and I'll talk about her any way I want."

"Not wit' me around, you won't," said Sonny, and he made a move toward rising from his chair.

Bert held him back with a firm hand on his forearm. Nacho barked. Citarella retreated half a step but tried to make it look like he hadn't. A couple of bodyguards slid closer. No one threw a punch or even managed a shove.

Ponte said, "Boys, boys, calm the fuck down. You're embarrassing me. Ya wanna talk trash, save it for the schoolyard. Frankie, sit the fuck down and don't bore us with your marital problems. We got grownup business to discuss."

Citarella took a seat as far away from Sonny as was

possible. Fat Lou, who'd briefly paused in his eating, got back to it. Livingstone just shook his head and looked down at his perfect fingernails.

Ponte crossed his pudgy hands in front of him and said, "Okay, gents, now that this preliminary bullshit is over with, let's get down to the main event. We're here to solve a problem. A major problem. Major enough that Lou here took the trouble to come down from New York, and Livingstone flew in all the way from Cape Town."

Bert said, "Cape Town? Where they shoot all the rockets off from?"

"That would be Cape Canaveral," said Livingstone. "This is Cape Town, South Africa. I take it you don't know much geography."

"No, not really," Bert admitted with a shrug.

"In any case," said Ponte, trying with mixed success not to sound exasperated, "let's review the situation. Until very recently, all of us, we had a good thing going. Livingstone was a reliable and trustworthy supplier—"

"Was?" the snooty man interjected. "*Is.* It's your side that's got it all bollixed up."

"Be that as it may," Ponte soldiered on, "until recently it was running pretty smooth. Supply from Africa. Importing through Key West. Distribution in New York. Something for each of us. Good money. Then some heat started coming down. Interpol, FBI, all the usual killjoys. So we all decided it'd be best to take a pause. Are we agreed on facts so far?"

Fat Lou grunted out a yes. Livingstone gave a grudging nod.

"So here's where it gets complicated," the host went on. "We're all feeling the heat, we're all getting a little paranoid, so, as of a couple months ago, we all clam up to play it safe, but this means that communication breaks down a little bit about exactly when the pause should start. So Livingstone's courier makes a last delivery but Lou's guy doesn't pick it up."

"He tried to pick it up," protested Lou, picking a bit of crab shell from between a couple molars. "But when he got there, the hot dog was all closed up, nobody around, so he figured the deal was off, so he left."

"Right. Okay," Bert the Shirt chimed in. "But *why* was the hot dog all closed up? It was closed up because Citarella here told Sonny that he should shut it down pronto and take it onna lam."

"Bullshit!" countered Citarella. "I did not say that. I told him there was one more pickup to be made. That he should sit tight for it, then close up."

"You're a fuckin' liar," Sonny said. "That isn't what you told me and you know it."

The wiry man ignored the comment. "So, what I think? I think Sonny here got scared. Lost his nerve. Bolted on us. Or I guess maybe there's one other possibility. Maybe he didn't lose his nerve. Maybe he found his nerve. Maybe he thought this was his chance to keep that shipment for himself."

Sonny twitched in his seat. Bert kept a hand on his arm.

"Or maybe *you* did," the old man countered. "Very convenient. Get Sonny outa town, tell Lou everything was off, then grab the package for yourself."

Citarella propped his elbows on the table and leaned across them. To the room at large, he said, "Who is this fucking fossil, and why's he even here?" When no one answered, he turned his eyes toward Bert again. "Look, you don't know shit about this. And now you have the balls t'accuse—"

Bert raised his hands in mock surrender. "I ain't accusin' nobody of nothin'. You're the one who started raisin' possibilities or ya might say various scenarios, so I'm raisin' a different one that happens to sound likelier than yours. Two months went by between that drop and now. Sonny was in New York. You live here in Florida. You coulda picked up the package at your leisure, like, say anytime ya came to Key West to do a little shoppin' wit' your lovely wife who you speak of wit' such chivalrous regard."

"You shut the fuck up about my wife. And cheese it on the crazy theories. All you're doin', you're trying to distract attention from how bad your pal Sonny fucked this whole thing up. First he blows it on the pick-up. Then he manages to lose the whole goddamn hot dog."

At that, there came half a beat of baffled silence that spread through the room like a bad odor.

Ponte litted a thick palm and said, "Hold on a sec. Did I just hear you say he lost the hot dog? The whole thing? Not just the shipment? The whole fucking wagon?"

Citarella glared at Sonny. Sonny glared back.

Livingstone shook his head again. "You people are unbelievable."

Bert said, "Yeah, you heard correct. The entire hot dog is AWOL. The frank, the bun, the wheels, the whole thing. Which was the bit of disappointin' news I hoped to present here in a calm and diplomatic manner before Citarella got his bowels in an uproar and just spit it out like a piece a rotten fruit."

Still chewing crabmeat, Fat Lou said, "How the hell'd you

guys lose the whole entire hot dog?"

"Look, I didn't lose it," Sonny said. "I came back exactly when Citarella told me to. The hot dog was there. The hot dog was fine. I saw it with my own eyes. But then I heard this cat, so—"

"Enough!" said Livingstone, and he smacked the table so violently that the chandelier above it trembled on its chain, though his expression never altered. "Listen, this arguing and blaming and these preposterous excuses about a cat are of no interest to me. None whatsoever. You seem to think this is all a game. But on my end of the business, we don't care for games. We take a more serious view. People die when they make mistakes. Sometimes even small mistakes. And someone here has made a big mistake. I couldn't care less which one of you it is. I don't care if it's both of you. And I don't care about your stupid hot dog. What I do care about is the package you seem to have lost. It's worth a lot of money. It's probably cost some lives already. I want it back. I want it back today."

He paused, tugged his shirt cuffs so that they were perfectly even, and adjusted his hat brim by some fraction of an inch. Then he glanced in turn at Ponte and Fat Lou. "Gentlemen," he went on, "your goodwill is valuable to me and I would hate to jeopardize it. So I'm asking your consent to what I believe is a fair and reasonable proposition. Either I get my package back by midnight, or these two bunglers will be eliminated. Is that acceptable to you?"

A moment passed. Bert rubbed Nacho's head. Sonny and Citarella stared at each other through slitted eyelids. Ponte and Fat Lou conferred with glances that just barely intersected.

Finally, the New York boss said, "I gotta agree that

someone messed up bad. Ya don't get your package, do what ya gotta do."

Ponte swallowed back heartburn and said, "It's a damn shame it's come to this, but yeah, okay, I'm in."

Citarella raised a hand as if preparing to protest, then seemed to realize there was nothing he could say.

Ponte exhaled and eased back in his seat. "Well, then, if there's nothing further—"

"'Scuse me," said Bert the Shirt, just as chair legs were beginning to scrape against the floor, "but before we adjourn and get on wit' the various and sundry business of our day, can I please just ask one very basic and possibly very dumb question?"

No one objected.

"So, um, Mr. Livingstone, or Dr. Livingstone if you prefer—"

"Just Livingstone, thank you."

"So, Livingstone, this package, upon which a very high and perhaps even fatalistic value has been placed, can I make bold t'ask just what the hell's inside of it?"

"You may ask. I won't tell you. You don't need to know."

"Well, um, I was just thinkin' it might make it a little bit easier to find it."

"No it wouldn't. Just find the package."

"Could I have a hint, at least? Ya know, inna name of fair play and all?"

"Fair play," said Livingstone in a disgusted tone. "There it is again. Like everything is just a game. Well, it isn't, and there won't be any hints." He looked down at his watch.

"Almost one o'clock. I strongly suggest you stop talking and start looking. Rest assured my men and I will be close by."

16

It started as a somber drive back down the Keys. No radio, no casual chit-chat, just the low whistling of the damp air through the rusted struts of the half-open convertible top, a sound that had now taken on the mournful quality of a receding train at night. Bert drove even slower than usual. Sonny stared absently at the looping telephone wires and the boats in the marinas. Even the dog was subdued, not leaning on the window frame and panting at the scenery, but quietly resting its chin on crossed paws in its master's lap.

At some point, just south of Islamorada, Sonny spoke for the first time in what felt like a long while. "Ya think he really means it?"

"He doesn't strike me as a whimsical guy," said Bert. "I don't think he kids around a lot."

The big man just pressed his lips together and nodded and went back to looking at the palm trees and the flashing water. A couple of miles passed before he spoke again, and when he did, his own words took him by surprise because they were not the kind of thing he'd ever even thought about before, let alone said out loud. "Jeez, Bert, today could be the last day of my life."

With both hands on the steering wheel and his eyes never straying from the dashed line in the middle of the road, the old man said softly, "Well, I got a little piece a news for ya, pal. So could any other day. Welcome to my world."

Sonny swallowed. It made his Adam's apple hurt.

"Don't look so glum about it," Bert went on. "Not the worst thing inna world to look it innee eye that the end could come at any time. Just like that. Boom, it's done. 'Zat a scary thought? Let's not bullshit here. 'Course it is. But it's kinda, whaddyacallit, liberatin' too. Calms ya down. Focuses the mind. Makes y'appreciate the little things. Someone smiles at ya, y'appreciate it. Somethin' makes ya laugh, it feels good, it's, like, a bonus. Somethin' goes wrong, fuck it, this bullshit too is gonna pass away. At least ya know ya won't have to deal wit' it forever. Makes ya kinda, ya know, philosophical."

Sonny scratched an ear. "Well, yeah, maybe I could come around to seein' it that way. Sorta. Eventually. If I live to get old. Not in one freakin' day, though."

"Fair enough. I guess it takes some time. It'd be askin' a lot to suddenly get comfy wit' the reaper onna basis of one stinkin' sitdown that didn't go so well."

"Went about as bad as anything could go."

"Well, yes and no," said Bert. "Death threat? Okay, net-net that's a minus. But at least we learned a couple things."

"We did? Like what the hell'd we learn?"

"Well, for one thing, we learned that Citarella has nothin' to gain by puttin' the blame on you, 'cause if Livingstone doesn't get his package, you're both equally screwed in a completely fifty-fifty and democratic way. It's not an either/or scenario like we thought it was. If you guys are goin' down, you're goin' down together."

"I don't really find that comforting," said Sonny.

"Nah, I guess it isn't. It wouldn't be like, say, Butch and

Sundance or Bonnie and Clyde, loyal comrades to the bitter end, which gives a little more dignity and whaddyacallit, pathos, I think the word is, to the story. But what it means is that, if Citarella took the wagon, which by this point I sincerely doubt but, what the hell, ya never know, he hands over the goods and hopefully no one gets hurt. Or, onnee other hand, if he's just as flummoxed as we are about the hot dog, he has just as much incentive to find it, so now we have what ya might call a two-pronged effort to locate the goods, which would be a plus. Plus we got quite a few hours left. Plus, on our side, we got a couple things that are definitely worth tryin'."

"We do? Like what?"

Bert took one hand off the wheel and gave the dozing chihuahua a few head-to-tail strokes before he answered. "We'll get to that," he said at last. "But first I wanna circle back a minute. I'm curious. I got a question for ya. So, say this really was the last day a your life. Not that I'm sayin' it will be. Not that I'm tryin' to make ya nervous. But, just for the sake a conversation as we toodle down the road, let's say it was. How would ya like to spend it?"

"How? Jeez." Sonny crossed his arms against his chest, then pulled in and let out an enormous breath. He closed his eyes, listened to the melancholy whistling of the breeze through the wrecked car roof, and pictured a few things he'd loved during a lifetime whose limited tenure he'd never really considered but that suddenly seemed radically foreshortened. He thought about cutting into big rare steaks, or being at the racetrack on a sunny afternoon, or just sitting on the stoop at dusk in the Brooklyn neighborhood where everybody knew his name. But as he wrestled with the monumental question of how he'd like to spend his final day, there was just a single standout wish. "I'd like to spend it wit'

Cecile," he said.

"Doin' what?" Bert asked.

"Well, not necessarily what you're prob'ly thinkin', though God knows I wouldn't mind that either. But mainly just bein' wit' her, lookin' at her, talkin'. Talkin' mostly. There's a few things I still don't understand, that I wish I understood a little better. Like why she broke up wit' me. Like if I did somethin' wrong, shoulda done somethin' different. I'd just like t'ask her."

"Think it would change how things turned out?"

The big man shrugged. "Nah, prob'ly not. I'd still be the guy who wasn't goin' nowhere, couldn't give her what she wanted. Prob'ly turn out just the same. Who knows? Anyway, what's the use? Not like it's gonna happen."

He went back to staring blankly out the window at the tiki huts and trailer parks and souvenir stands stocked with seashells and racks of candy-colored flip-flops. Bert kept quiet and drove very slowly to Key West, stopping now and then to use the restroom, walk the dog, and make a couple phone calls.

17

Deep in conversation or lost in reverie, neither Bert nor Sonny noticed that one of the many cars that went whizzing past them on U.S. 1 belonged to Frankie Citarella, who was driving his Mercedes at a breakneck pace, weaving in and out of lanes, playing chicken with red lights, passing RV's on the right and spitting gravel from the shoulder of the road. The wiry man drove so hard that he'd made it all the way to the Cow Key Bridge while the ancient El Dorado was still lumbering along through Key deer territory; but when he screeched onto the A1A and went careening on two wheels around the curve before the airport, he was moving so fast that he saw nothing but a hectic blur of intertwining mangroves with not the slightest hint of a clearing in the midst of them. He sped along the length of Smathers Beach and finally came to a rocking halt at curbside between the food trucks and the public showers.

Hands cramped from the steering wheel, shiny shirt pasted against his sweaty back, he got out of the car, stretched himself, and started making inquiries about the mysterious disappearance of the hot dog wagon. He asked at the pizza stand. All they knew was that it was there one day and gone the next. He asked at the taco truck. They hadn't heard of any plan to roll the thing away. He learned nothing from the ice-cream man, nothing from the Sno-cone lady.

Thwarted, he sat down on the seawall. It was getting close to five o'clock by then. There was hardly anyone on the beach except a few people who'd fallen asleep there and would be blistered or peeling by tomorrow. The sunlight was softening to butter yellow and the shadows were getting longer; even the little ridges in the sand threw shadows, like tiny dunes trailing purple twins. The temperature dropped a few degrees and Citarella's sweaty shirt felt clammy.

At some point, a rangy, stringy man came walking down the promenade. He was wearing cutoff jeans with strings hanging down both legs, and a torn-up denim shirt with holes in the elbows. The sole of one of his sandals flopped when he walked. He was carrying a rolled up towel that had no loops left in the terry-cloth and he was heading toward the open-air showers. When he got there, he stepped out of his shoes, pulled off his shirt, revealing lean but ropy arms and shoulders, and started the flow of tepid water. He drenched his head, scrubbed his torso with a skinny and diminishing piece of soap, and tried discreetly to clean himself inside his shorts.

When the rangy man was lathered up, Citarella approached him, standing just outside the misty rainbow of the shower spray. "Hey, fella, can I talk to you a minute? Might be worth your while."

The man was not at first concerned as he looked up from his washing. It was not unusual to be talked to at the outdoor showers. When the regulars were around, there was usually some banter and some joking going on. Sometimes the tourists were chatty, too. Now and then it could get a little creepy, but by and large people were just friendly. No harm in it. "Yeah, sure," he said.

Citarella did his best to flash a winning smile. "Cool. Thanks. What's your name?"

"Pineapple."

"Pineapple? That's a new one on me. Never met anybody by that name before."

Piney shrugged and started rinsing off. He was just beginning to have some faint misgivings about this conversation with a stranger who was not dressed for the beach, though his first thought was that the wiry man might be some sort of plainclothes cop. "Look, I didn't bring shampoo," he said.

"Shampoo?"

"I know it's against the rules," said Piney. "That's why I don't do it. All I got's this little piece of soap." He held forth the shrinking sliver as evidence.

Puzzled, Citarella said, "Listen, shampoo, no shampoo, I don't give a rat's ass. I'm not looking for shampoo. What I'm looking for is information."

"Information?" echoed Pineapple, his stomach now starting to knot up. "Sorry, mister, that's not anything I'm good at. I'm pretty bad at information." He kept on rinsing.

Citarella frowned then reached into a pocket and came out with a fat billfold. The billfold had a silver clip that flashed hellishly in the low sunlight, and the wad of money had an illicit and trouble-bringing look that made Piney just want to get out of there. He turned off the shower and reached for his towel. The towel didn't absorb much anymore and it was wet before half of him was dry. He pulled his shirt on anyway and was stepping into his sandals when Citarella said, "You hang out here a lot, Pineapple?"

"No, not really, not a lot. From time to time."

The wiry man peeled off a twenty and held it dangling in space as he pointed with his chin toward the broken line of food trucks. "You know the hot dog wagon that used to be there?"

"Well, yeah, I sort of remember it, sure."

Citarella licked his thumb and peeled off another bill, stacking it on top of the first. "Know anything about how it disappeared?"

Piney tried to speak but the lie stuck in his throat a moment. Finally, he said, "Um, no. Why would I?"

More money was unfurled from the evil-looking bankroll. "Means a lot to me to find it."

"How come?" Piney couldn't help himself from asking. "I mean, it's yours?"

Citarella, no longer bothering to act friendly, pulled his lips back from his teeth and said, "I have the money, Pineapple, which means I get to ask the questions. You don't even understand that much?"

"No, I guess I don't."

"So listen, I will ask you one more time. You know anything about where that fucking hot dog is?"

Piney didn't want to have to lie out loud a second time. He gathered up his towel and his scrap of soap and just said, "Sorry, mister, I can't help you."

Citarella scowled and put the wad back in his pocket. "You better not be jerking me around," he said.

Pineapple didn't answer, just took a half-step up the

promenade toward the clearing in the mangroves before the instinct of caution counseled him to walk the other way. He pivoted on his flopping shoes and took a very long and labored route to get back home.

🌴 🌴 🌴

Twenty minutes later, Bert finally pulled into his garage.

The archaic Caddy shuddered like a played-out horse as the ignition was switched off; a blob of thick blue liquid leaked out of the transmission and streamed along the cement floor. Dodging the line of goo, the old man and his dog and their houseguest went upstairs to the condo, where the first thing Bert did was to retrieve his wife's dainty opera glasses from the end table with the sticking drawer.

He carried them over to the living room window, brushed the curtain aside with an elbow, and peered down at the roadway and the promenade below. Joggers in tank tops and skaters with knee pads, having waited out the heat of the day, were now streaming along the beachfront path. Sunset-watchers in bright hats were carrying chairs and coolers toward the water's edge. And a bedraggled Frankie Citarella was just getting up from the seawall and walking with a discouraged posture toward his car.

Maybe fifteen yards beyond his Mercedes, two black SUVs were parked along the curb. Leaning back against each vehicle was a pair of goons in Ray-Bans, arms crossed in such a way as to make their biceps look tremendous. Through the blue-tinted glass of the lead car, the profile of a man with a hat-brim pulled low and at a jaunty angle could just barely be distinguished.

"Looks like Livingstone came down wit' some extra

muscle," the old man said. "Two teams. Guy's efficient, ya gotta give 'im that. Have a look?"

Sonny took the glasses. He saw Citarella climb into his Benz and ease away from curbside. The lead SUV, without even a token nod to stealth, pulled away to tail him. That left one pair of killers to keep an eye on the Paradiso condo. Sonny put the glasses down and said, "So what the hell we do from here?"

Bert had settled into his favorite threadbare armchair with the doilies on the arms and the wrinkled antimacassar behind his head. He stole a quick look at his watch and said, "Well, for starters, I was hopin' maybe ya could do me a favor."

"Sure, Bert. Anything."

"I was hopin' maybe ya could do a load a wash."

Sonny wasn't quite sure he'd heard right. "Wash?"

"Yeah, ya know, laundry. Over at the laundromat. It'd really help me out. I'm pretty much to the bottom a the drawer on socks and hankies."

The big man fumbled for an answer to the odd request. He owed Bert a lot. He'd just said he'd do anything. Still, with his life expectancy now measured in hours as opposed to years, doing laundry just didn't seem like the best use of his time. He briefly wondered if his friend and counselor had picked this worst possible moment to go soft in the head.

For some seconds neither man spoke. Bert just sat there scratching his dog between the ears. Finally he went on. "Diversionary tactic. Get it? Basic. Fundamental. The goombahs follow you as you head out wit' the laundry basket. I get to slip away and run a little errand. *Capeesh?*"

18

So Sonny headed out on foot for the laundromat a handful of blocks away on White Street, holding against his chest a cracked plastic basket bristling with the toes of dirty socks and the dangling shoulder straps of Bert's old-fashioned undershirts. The sun had just set and the streetlamps buzzed as they were warming up; the light was a grainy mix of lavender dusk and pink-orange gleam. The breeze off the ocean was salty and cool but the pavement was still soft from the heat of afternoon. The black SUV idled along fifty feet behind him on Atlantic Boulevard. He didn't have to look around to know it was still there.

On White Street he sauntered past the bocce courts and the bodega where old Cubans still played dominoes on flattened cardboard boxes, and then he came to the laundromat called Duds and Suds. The place had a roof but no front wall; it was wide open to the street, and since, in Key West, it seemed only normal that a laundromat should also be a bar, there was a counter and some beer taps and an adequate selection of booze bottles and glassware laid out on a couple of shelves, and, just to the left of the rank of dryers, a few small tables with blue umbrellas.

Sonny found an empty washing machine, fumbled with the change and detergent dispensers, and started the load.

Then he ordered a beer and sat down at a table. He could clearly see his stalkers parked across the street but he felt surprisingly safe and cozy in the laundromat. Maybe it was the comforting smell of fresh warm lint, or maybe the peaceful music in the soft whir of the spin cycle.

He sipped his beer. Light traffic criss-crossed White Street. Bicycles went by. Then a neon-lighted pedi-cab pulled up, and from it stepped the most beautiful woman Sonny had ever seen. She was wearing tall white shoes with heel-straps, a short tight skirt with a leopard-spot design, and a black blouse that glimmered against her ample collarbones and was open well beyond the throat. Her hair was swept up high and windproof, her carmine lipstick overflowed the outline of her lips, and her eyebrows were two emphatic chevrons. He watched as she placed an adorable, plump foot on the pavement. He watched her long red fingernails as she paid the driver. Not sure if she was real or just a vision granted him on the last day of his life, he stood up and called, "Cecile!"

She turned and smiled at him. He could hardly believe it. She more than smiled; she beamed. "Sonny!" She took a firm step up to sidewalk level and breezed toward him, her arms spread open for a chaste but thrilling hug. "Those flowers you sent, they were just so beautiful!"

"They were?"

"And the chocolates!"

"Um, the chocolates. Right."

"Just like you used to do. Those little boxes. Six assorted pieces. So considerate. So romantic. Jeez, it's good to see you, Sonny. How'd you even know I was in town, where I was staying?"

"Well, uh, I—"

"Oh, hey, it doesn't matter. We're here, that's what counts. Jeez, it's just so good to see you. Big and strong and sweet as ever. So much to catch up on. Buy a girl a drink?"

Dizzy from her presence and the hug and her vanilla-scented perfume, he swayed a little where he stood and mumbled, "Sure, yeah. Whaddya feel like?"

"Oh, come on. You don't remember?"

"Sure I do. Course I do. Thought you mighta changed it up by now."

"No. I really haven't changed much, Sonny. Some ways maybe. Not in others. Most ways I'm just the same."

He wafted to the counter to order her a sweet vermouth with an orange slice. She took a seat and glanced around at total strangers standing elbow to elbow as they folded their boxers and their bras, their negligees and thongs.

"Perfect place you picked," she said when he returned. "Different. Kind of intimate with all these people airing out their dirty laundry. Cheers!"

They clinked glasses. Sonny, tongue-tied, just said, "I can't believe you're here with me, Cecile."

"How could I not come, with that beautiful note you sent?"

"Um, the one with the flowers and the chocolates?"

"It was beautiful. So tell me, Sonny. How've you been? Where've you been? You happy? You with anyone?"

"Happy? Sometimes. With anyone? No, not really."

"A nice guy like you?"

He shrugged. Behind him, quarters were slipping

through coin slots and dropping into metal boxes with a muted clang; there was the ca-chunk of wash cycles kicking in. "Haven't been that interested, I guess. Haven't felt, ya know, the spark."

She took a pull of her vermouth. "Ah, the spark. I remember that. Well, least you have your freedom. More than I can say."

"You got Frankie."

"Thanks for reminding me."

"Besides, it's not like havin' my freedom woulda been my first choice anyway. My first choice was you, Cecile. Just didn't work out that way."

She said nothing, just lowered her eyes so that the lashes threw long shadows down across her cheeks.

He sipped some beer, started to speak, stopped himself, then figured what the hell, how many chances like this came along in life, even in a life that wasn't suddenly cut short? "Can I ask you something, though?" he said at last "When you left me for Frankie...well, why? How'd I mess up? I mean, I know he's smarter, more ambitious—"

"You didn't mess up, Sonny. But the ambition thing, I guess that was part of it, just not in a way I'm proud of. I like stuff, what can I say? New stuff, nice stuff, fancy stuff. At least I used to like it. At least I thought I did. I thought it would make me happy. And yeah, I figured Frankie could give me more of that. But, ya know, I wasn't just being selfish. Mostly maybe. But I was thinking about you, too. Didn't want to stick you with a life that wasn't right for you. Having to make money, worry about moving up—"

"I don't mind working, Cecile."

"I know you don't, but come on, Sonny, let's be real. I'm

not stupid. I know the world Frankie lives in. Guys get hurt. Guys end up in prison. I didn't want that for you. I thought without me bugging you for clothes and shoes and furniture, well, I thought you'd have a better chance of getting out. Or maybe that was just an excuse I told myself. Who knows? Hard to tell if you're really being honest with yourself. Gotta try though, right? Anyway, turns out all that nice new stuff hasn't made me happy. It's made me miserable, ya want the truth. Can I have another drink?"

He stood up to fetch another round. She dabbed at her eyes and watched other people's shirts and nighties turning in the dryers, somersaulting weightlessly as astronauts.

He brought the drinks and sat again. "I'm sorry you're not happy, baby. I really am."

She managed a small smile and said, "Baby. You called me Baby."

"Did I? Didn't mean to. Just slipped out."

"It's okay. It was nice. Been a while since I heard it. Been awhile since I heard anything nice. Been awhile since I said anything nice, ya wanna know the truth. I've been awful to him, Sonny. A real pain lately. Not fair, I admit it. It's like I'm taking it out on him that I just don't know what I want. It's really not his fault. He is who he is. He's trying."

Sonny sipped some beer. "I guess he is. But, ya know, it's funny, I useta really like the guy. We were friends. Not, okay, like best friends, but we got along just fine. Then he takes you away from me. So which one of us has the right to be mad? Call me crazy, I think it's me. But he's the one who suddenly seems to have a grudge. I've just never understood it."

Cecile drank some of her vermouth then carefully

centered her glass on its soggy cardboard coaster. Very softly, she said, "I do. I understand it. I understand it 'cause it's my fault."

"Your fault? Don't blame yourself, Cecile. It's between two knuckleheaded guys."

"Yes and no." She paused then took in a long, slow breath and leaned low across the table. "Listen, Sonny, I really shouldn't tell you this, it's probably not so ladylike, but with all the dirty laundry in this place, what the hell? So what happened was that it was the first time Frankie was making love to me, and everything was going fine, and then, kind of right before the big moment, which by the way turned out not to be so big a moment, but anyway, right before what I thought was gonna be the big moment...well, I made a really dumb mistake. I said your name."

"You did?"

She was blushing. To Sonny it made her still more beautiful. "Not your whole name. I caught myself. I just sort of said Suh...But that was enough. Frankie heard it. He knew where it was going. I couldn't pull it back. So he knows I still have it for you, Sonny. And he hates you for it."

"Jeez, musta been hard for 'im to hear that. I can't help feelin' kinda bad for the guy."

"That's 'cause you're a sweetheart. Some men would just be gloating, don'tcha think?"

"Well, maybe there's a tiny bit of that, too," he admitted.

"So, anyway," she said, "I've put myself in a helluva situation. Married to a guy who knows deep down I'm still in love with someone else. Someone I treated really unfair, broke up with for a stupid reason, who there's no way he would take me back in a million years even if I wasn't married."

Washing machines were laboring and sloshing. Dryers purred. Sonny said, "You think he wouldn't? Who says he wouldn't?"

Cecile looked up from under her lashes. "You think he would? You think he might?"

"In a heartbeat, Cecile. If it's what you wanted. If you were sure. In a heartbeat."

She picked up her drink, put it down without drinking, took one of Sonny's hands in both of hers. "Oh my God," she said, "Really? I can't believe this is really happening. I can't even tell if I'm laughing or crying. It's so crazy, so romantic, so sudden. In a laundromat, for Chrissake! I'm just giddy, Sonny. I don't know what I should do. No, I do know what I should do. I should follow my heart this time. I should be honest with myself. I should call Frankie and tell him it's over. Tell him I'm leaving him. I should do it right now. Get it over with."

"Well, um, maybe you should save it for tomorrow."

Her beaming face darkened. "Tomorrow? Why, Sonny? You have doubts? You want an out?"

"I don't have doubts. I'm sure. But listen, I don't want you should worry, but Frankie and me are in some trouble. Both of us. A lotta trouble, actually. Tonight could get pretty hairy. Me, I'm the happiest guy in the world right now, knowin' that you're comin' back to me. World ends tonight, I'm happy. So why make Frankie miserable if it turns out not to matter?"

"Not to matter? But—"

"Look, Cecile, do I have to spell it out? Frankie and me, tomorrow might or might not happen."

She pressed her knuckles against her lips. "That stupid fucking crooked life. That's why I wanted you out of it."

"And I will be. As of midnight. One way or the other. That's a promise."

They sat without speaking for a moment. Coins clanged. Buzzers buzzed. Then Cecile leaned low across the table and said, "Will you kiss me, Sonny?"

"It'd be okay?" he asked. "Wit' you still bein' a married lady and all?"

"Just once. Let's see if the spark's still there."

They kissed, the old thrill of it lifting them halfway off their seats. It was not a long kiss. It didn't need to be. The first light brushing of their lips was enough to bring back everything they'd missed.

"You take good care tonight," was all she said when the kiss was over. She grabbed her purse, all but floated to the curb, and hailed a pedi-cab to go back to the hotel.

Sonny sat there for a dazed and blissful moment then got up to move Bert's laundry to a dryer.

19

Meg and Peter had just sat down to what they hoped would be a serene and simple poolside dinner, the sort of modest but civilized ritual that they'd taken for granted until mere days ago, but which had suddenly come to seem a rare and exotic treat. There were candles on the table set for two. The cat was curled up under Peter's chair. The wine had been poured, the obligatory clink of glasses duly honored. The salmon had just come off the grill and Peter's first flaky forkful was halfway to his lips, when the doorbell rang.

By a dutiful reflex, Meg immediately started getting up to answer it.

Peter said, "Oh for Christ's sake, it's dinnertime. Can we please just let it ring?"

"What if it's important?"

"What if it's two Mormons in skinny ties?"

"What if someone needs our help?"

"What if someone doesn't? Most people seem to be managing just fine without us."

She let him have the last word but she went to answer the door. Peter ate some salmon and a couple bites of farro salad while she was away, but the interruption made the food less tasty.

She was back in a minute with Bert the Shirt in tow, cradling Nacho against his belly until he was sure the dog and the Kaplans' cat would get along. The animals briefly glanced at one another. Sasha purred. Nacho wriggled. Bert lowered him to the deck. Cat and dog approached and sniffed each other like new arrivals from separate planets then almost immediately lost interest. Meg made a place for Bert and asked if he'd like some dinner. He declined. She offered him a glass of wine. He accepted. Then, glancing at the candles and the food already on the plates, he said, "Jeez, I'm awful sorry bargin' in like this."

"Hey, it's no problem," said Meg. From her it sounded honest, though from Peter it would obviously have been a fib. Then again, what else could they say to a very old man whom they'd known for quite a while, and who had never before in all the years of their acquaintanceship just popped over unannounced at dinnertime? "What's up?" she went on.

Bert settled into his chair and sipped some wine. "Well, it's hard to know exactly how or where to start, or to begin or commence as you might say, but basically, to cut to the chase, it sort of has somethin' to do wit' your cat, who, as I understand it or at least have been informed, has been actin' very weird of late."

"You're telling me?" said Peter. "She's been acting like she's lost her mind. Unspayed jungle cat. Insane. But what's it go to do with you?"

"Wit' me? Directly? Nothin'. But you guys and me, well, we have this mutual acquaintance. Ya know who I mean. Sonny."

At the mere mention of the name, Sasha lifted her head and panned eagerly all across the yard as if the beloved visitor might suddenly reappear.

Putting down his fork and gesturing toward the cat, Peter said, "You see? You see? She's lost her mind."

"Well, anyway," said Bert, "where I'm goin' wit' this is that our friend Sonny is in a tight spot on accounta he lost his hot dog, and last night, very late at night, he was outside contemplatin' or ya might say broodin' on his situation, and then the cat comes along and starts actin' very strange, and then, well, wit' due respect and no value judgment implied 'cause I'm just passin' along how it seemed to Sonny...then you, Peter, you come along and *you* start actin' very strange."

"Strange?" said Peter, who'd gone back to eating salmon but was beginning to have a bit of trouble swallowing his food. "I wasn't acting strange. How was I acting strange?"

"Well, look," said Bert, "I wasn't there, I ain't takin' a position. But what Sonny tells me is that the cat is sniffin' its way along the curb, startin' from where the hot dog used to be, and he's, Sonny I mean, he's curious, and you're nervous, and then more nervous, and then somewhere gettin' close up by the airport, you sorta get a runnin' start and take a flyin' header and tackle the cat."

Meg was sipping wine but quickly lowered her glass. "You tackled the cat?"

"I didn't tackle the cat. I...so, what happened was—"

"You told me you tripped. You didn't tell me you tackled her."

"Well, I did trip. Sort of."

The old man's gaze flicked back and forth between husband and wife, then he said, "Look, tripped, slipped, dove, fell, whatever. Point is, your pj's got wrecked but now at least you have the cat. But the part that Sonny couldn't help wonderin' about—well, it's two things really. The first thing, or let's call it part A just to keep it nice and simple, is whether there was even a snowball's chance in hell that what the cat was doin' was trackin' down the hot dog, which who knows if a cat's brain even works that way. Which brings us to the second thing he wondered about, which for the sake a clarity we will call part B, namely, he was wonderin' if it was just remotely possible that you too, Peter, were wonderin' if the cat was sniffin' its way toward the hot dog wagon, but that maybe, for whatever reason known only to yourself and wit'out castin' any aspersions whatsoever, ya didn't wanna let it happen."

"But that's ridiculous," said Peter. "Why wouldn't I?"

"Well, I dunno," the old man said. "That's kinda what I come over t'ask ya."

"Look, it was the middle of the night. I was tired. I wanted to go home."

"Completely unnerstandable. But that reminds me. So you and Sonny and the cat go back down the promenade, and he walks you to your car so you can go back home, but your car is all dinged up and scratched, which he was pretty sure it wasn't a day or two before—"

"Bert, enough already. What's with the third degree?"

The old man hesitated. Meg poured out more wine. Peter made a halfhearted stab at his salmon but the hand that held the fork was shaking a bit and he pushed his plate away.

"Listen," said Bert the Shirt. "I'm sorry. I really am. I interrupt your dinner, I pester ya wit' all these questions. But it isn't, whaddyacallit, frivolous, I promise. Sonny's in real trouble."

"What kind of trouble?" asked Meg. "How bad?"

Bert tugged at the placket of his forest green silk shirt. "Sorry, but I can't go into that right now. I mean, ya gotta understand. We got a code about these things."

"But you're asking us for help," she said.

"That's true, I am."

"And you're putting Peter in the middle of something very uncomfortable. Does that seem fair to you, Bert?"

He reached under the table, swept his dog into his lap, and stroked its head a moment. "Fair, unfair, I don't really know. God knows I never wanna be unfair. I'm just tryin' to help out a friend, not put anyone onna spot."

"But you are," Meg quietly insisted.

"Yeah, I guess I am, but believe me, I wouldn't do it unless it was important. So please, can I just ask one more simple question, yes or no?" He fixed his deep black eyes on Peter's. "Do you know where the hot dog is?"

Peter's mouth twitched at one corner and he said, "Well, um—"

"Yes, he does," said Meg. "So do I. He's told me. And we have a pretty good reason for not wanting anyone else to find out."

The old man scratched the dog. "Okay, fair enough. I thank you for your, whaddyacallit, straightforwardness and candor. So, now that we've arrived at this hopeful moment of trust and frankness, may I please inquire what your reason is?"

Peter sat with his mouth half open and his twitchy gaze fixed on his wife.

Meg slowly shook her head. "Sorry, Bert, you can't. I mean, ya gotta unnerstand. We got a code about these things."

"A code," the old man said. "Okay, touché. So you also got a code. My code, your code, I guess the two codes balance out. Looks like it might be time to lay the cards out onna table."

20

By the time Pineapple made it back to the clearing, the sky was fully dark except for the bright but smudgy pinpricks of the misted stars, and the campfire where Fred was keeping dinner warm had mostly burned down to a ring of pulsing coals. "Jeez, Piney," he said, "what took you so long? Hours, I mean. I thought you were just goin' for a shower."

"I was. I did. Something kind of scary happened."

Fred looked more closely at his friend in the dim firelight. Piney's usually placid face was crinkled at the edges of his eyes; his cheeks were hollow and he kept shifting his weight from one leg to the other. "You okay?"

"I'm awful tired, Fred. And my feet are hurtin' somethin' bad. And I'm a little worried that I mighta really messed us up. I hope I didn't, but I mighta. So I'm a little worried."

Softly, in a tone that he would never in a thousand lifetimes admit was tender, almost motherly, Fred said, "I bet you didn't mess us up. Come on, how 'bout we get you off your feet and have our ravioli and you can tell me all about it."

So Piney eased down onto a fireside rock, his legs

stretched out in front of him, his back to the hot dog with its open service window and the starlight twinkling on the mustard squiggle. Fred handed him a tin can with the label singed off and his canteen full of water, then he popped himself a beer. Times like this, Piney almost wished he could drink again. Almost but not quite.

"So what happened?" asked his friend.

Famished though he was, Pineapple still ate slowly. He forked a single raviolo then launched in. "Well, I was in the shower, and this guy comes along and starts asking me questions. What my name is. Do I hang around there. Then he starts takin' out money. Offers me a twenty."

"A twenty? Tryin' to get you into one of the bathroom stalls?"

"Nah, it wasn't anything like that. He starts asking me about the hot dog. Like, did I remember it? When did I first notice it was missing? Said he'd make it worth my while if I could give him any information. And the whole time, he's peeling off more cash. But ya know what really scared me? The clip that held the money."

"The clip?"

"This big, clunky, shiny silver thing. It made me think of when Peter was here and talking about the trouble we were in, and saying maybe it was Mafia, and you and me, well, you especially, were pooh-poohing it, like what's the Mafia want with little old Key West? What's the Mafia want with a broken down old hot dog truck? But when I saw that money clip, I thought holy cow, it's for real, it's Mafia. I mean I just couldn't imagine a regular person carrying around a money clip like that. So I got really nervous and I told him I didn't know anything. But you know what a bad liar I am, Fred, so I figured he saw right through me and now he knew I must be hiding something."

Fred finished his beer and crumpled up the can. "So he kept after ya? He asked more questions?"

"I didn't stick around to find out. I put my shirt on and left. Wasn't even dried off yet. But then I made a really dumb mistake. I started walking straight toward home. Up the promenade. Then I thought, wait, that's the dumbest thing I could do. So, really quick, I changed direction. But now I'm wondering did I do it quick enough? Did it look weird that I took a half-step one way then suddenly spun around the other way? Did he notice? So then I started imagining he was following me. I couldn't let myself turn around to check. I was afraid it would look suspicious. So I just kept walking, getting more jumpy, even wishing a little bit that we still slept on the ground instead of having all this trouble. So I took this crazy route all down through Bahama Village and up a couple alleys, just to shake him off if he was following. Then I went way out by the Coast Guard base and around the City docks, so I don't even know how long I've been walking. I just hope I didn't mess us up."

Fred put his empty tin of food aside and kicked at the campfire to make some sparks. Trying to sound reassuring, he said, "Can't imagine anyone would follow you that far on foot. And no one could do it in a car. Not with all those alleys. I don't think you messed up, Piney."

He looked up from his half-finished tin of ravioli. "Well, I hope not. But if I did...well, would you be mad at me, Fred?"

"Mad at ya? No, Piney, I wouldn't be mad. I mean, shit happens. Things go wrong sometimes."

"So we'd still be friends?"

"Course we would. Dead friends maybe. But friends."

"Okay, thanks. I just had to ask. You know me, Fred. Sometimes I get a little emotional if I'm really tired."

"Don't worry about it. Look, ya didn't answer the guy's questions. Ya led him on a wild goose chase. Ya did good."

Seeming satisfied with that, Pineapple went back to eating very slowly. Fred popped another beer. But as he sat there drinking it, he started getting worried, just a little bit at first, but then the worry took on a kind of sandpapery insistence that just kept scratching at his peace of mind. It was true that Piney was the world's worst liar; his whole face changed on the rare occasions when he told a lie; a Mafia guy, of all people, could probably read it easily. And what about that first unthinking step in the direction of home? What if the Mafia guy was savvy enough to go snooping up that way, rather than falling for the complicated detour?

Uneasy now, Fred silently stood up and climbed into the hot dog. He returned a moment later bearing his machete and, as the closest thing he could find to a weapon for Piney, a long steel grill fork whose tines were slightly mangled. Sitting down by the fire again, and as if there'd been no break in the conversation, he said, "Never hurts to be prepared, though. Just in case this joker happens to show up."

Pineapple set aside his food and glanced doubtfully at the giant fork. "Fred," he said, "what the heck am I supposed to do that?"

"Hopefully, nothing. Worse comes to worse, well, you know, stick 'im with it."

"Like a piece of meat? Both prongs? I don't think I could do that, Fred."

"If it was him or you?"

The tall man scratched an eyebrow. "So I guess you really do think I messed up."

"I didn't say that, Piney. I'm just saying let's defend ourselves. Let's be ready."

They sat a while longer but Pineapple's stomach had knotted up and he no longer felt like finishing his dinner. Fred had one more beer and pretended to be calm. The night got both quieter and louder, the distant sounds of cars and scooters diminishing as the rasping of crickets and bleating of toads grew bolder. The ocean smelled closer as the sunbaked daytime aroma of the mangroves faded. At some point fatigue trumped nervousness, and Piney yawned. Five seconds later, so did Fred.

That was the drowsy moment when they heard a car that seemed to be moving much more slowly than the others that had scudded by on A1A.

They were unconcerned at first as they listened to the subtly rising pitch of its approach, but grew alert when they didn't hear the falling note of its retreat. A moment later, from the direction of where their secret little pathway joined the road, came the abruptly dying sound of a switched-off engine.

Fred was on his feet by then, the machete clutched in his right hand, his fingers wriggling on the hilt, his ears cocked toward the unsettling sounds. He heard two dry clicks of car doors being opened, then two muffled slams as they were closed again. Whispering now, he said to Piney, "That guy who talked to you. He was alone?"

Feeling shame at messing up even more than he was feeling fear, he said, "I think so, Fred. I didn't see anybody else."

"Sounds like he's got help now. Come on, get up. Grab the fork."

The tall man rose reluctantly, his lean face ashen, the grotesque utensil dangling limply from his hand. Fred bounded over and took up a position at a corner of the wagon. Piney followed, moving as though his joints were fused. They heard a faint rustling and snap of fallen twigs from the road end of the path.

A heartbeat later, Fred urgently rasped out, "No, this spot's no good. They'll probably have guns. We try to fight 'em from a distance, we're fucked. Gotta duck down right at the edge of the clearing. Get 'em before they can even see in the dark. Hack first, ask questions later."

He scampered over and crouched behind a mangrove, gesturing to Piney to stake out the other side of the path just where it began to widen out. "I don't think I can do this," he said again in a quavering whisper.

Fred didn't answer, just limbered up his arm and raised the machete to shoulder height. Piney fiddled with the grill fork, tried to get it settled in his sweating palm. The rustle of leaves and snap of twigs got louder, closer.

Fred tightened down his jaw and lifted the machete high above his head, poised to strike, ready to hack. Piney began silently to weep. Footsteps neared the fatal spot where the path opened to the clearing.

The machete whistled as it started to come down.

And a voice just then was calling out, "Piney! Fred! It's Peter and Meg. We have some wonderful news for you!"

21

"She loves me!" Sonny sang out, the instant Bert and Nacho got home from their diplomatic mission to the Kaplans'. The big man was folding Bert's laundry and stacking it neatly on the living room sofa. His thick hands were surprisingly good at getting the pleats and creases just exactly right. "She loves me," he went on, "and I know it, and whatever happens, no one can take that away from me, and I owe it all to you."

"Baloney," said the old man, as he bent to let his chihuahua off the leash. "You don't owe me nothin'. She loves ya 'cause you're true blue, that's why she loves ya. 'Cause ya never blamed her. 'Cause ya never got bitter. 'Cause ya never gave up."

Sonny came out with a quick wonderstruck laugh as he worked. "And me, I'm thinkin' what the fuck is up wit' doin' laundry on the last night a my life? Totally deked me, Bert. I gotta hand it to ya. But the flowers, the chocolates—that was genius. When'd'ya even have time to do all that?"

"All those pit-stops on the way back from Ponte's. Ya think all I did was pee?"

"And the note. She said the note was beautiful. You made the note up on the fly?"

"Nah, I asked the concierge to write somethin' nice. Figured he could manage it. He sounded like the romantic type. Concierges usually are. S'anyway, I'm glad it worked, glad she's seen the light."

Sonny suddenly choked up and all he could do at first was nod. "It's like a miracle," he managed. "Almost too good to be true."

"So she went back to dump that slimeball Citarella?"

"I asked her not to tell him till tomorrow. Why rub the poor guy's face in it if it isn't gonna matter anyway?"

"Very thoughtful of ya," Bert said, "but guess what? It's lookin' like this guy's gonna live plenty long enough to know he's dumped and you're gonna live long enough to have a honeymoon wit' your sweetie."

"I am? What the hell makes you so confident?"

Bert said nothing for a moment, just went over and retrieved his dead wife's opera glasses and looked out the window to where Livingstone's killers were again parked at the curb. Then he glanced down at his watch. "Ten-thirty," he announced. "We're gonna beat the deadline wit' a little time to spare. Think I'll chill a bottle a Prosecco. Meg and Peter should be here any minute."

"Meg and Peter?" Sonny said. "What the hell do they have to do with it?" He kept on folding laundry. The dog jumped up on the sofa, hoping that the two of them could play a little. Sonny pushed him off. The dog jumped up again.

By then Bert had gone into the kitchen and was putting a bottle in the freezer. Matter-of-factly, he yelled out, "Well, they know where the hot dog is."

"They what?"

The old man came back into the living room. "The hot dog. They know where it is. They've known all along. Peter has, at least."

Sonny paused in his folding. "They knew all along? And they didn't have the decency to tell me? Even when they knew I was sweatin' bullets over it? Even when I was right there in their house?"

"Well, it's complicated. Ya gotta see both sides. Not always easy in life, but ya gotta try. Ya see, they have an obligation. There's a couple people they're protectin'. This I understand. This I respect. So we talked the whole thing through and, after a few rounds of the typical you-show-me-yours-and-I'll-show-ya-mine, we reached what I believe to be a fair and equitable, and one might even say a whaddyacallit, Solomaniac compromise."

He broke off and began the gradual and cautious process of settling into his favorite armchair. Then he slowly crossed his shrunken legs. Then he pulled a handkerchief from a back pocket and creakily leaned forward to rub away a scuff on his left shoe.

Sonny said, "So what the hell's the compromise?"

"I thought you'd never ask. The compromise is that they wouldn't tell me where the hot dog is 'cause they didn't wanna get their friends in trouble, but they agreed to go pick up Livingstone's precious package, which their friends probably wouldn't even know about and wouldn't have any interest in anyway. So here comes the beauty part. They bring the package over here and I hand it off to the goons. Livingstone gets his shipment of whatever and gets the hell outa town. These unknown friends get the hot dog, which no one else gives a flyin' crap about, for a place to live. You get Cecile, the Kaplans get a good night's sleep, and everybody's happy 'cept that scumbag Citarella, but fuck 'im. So, pretty sweet outcome all in all."

Sonny could do nothing but shake his head in awe. "Pretty sweet? It's more than pretty sweet, Bert. It's amazing. And you figured all that out in just one day, on toppa handlin' the sitdown? On toppa settin' everything up wit' Cecile and me? That's like unbelievable."

Modestly, the old man said, "I had a pretty good day. Nice ta feel I still got a few a those left in me." He crossed his hands in his lap and dozed off momentarily.

Still shaking his head and chuckling very softly, the big man went back to folding laundry. But then, when he had almost reached the bottom of the basket, he came across the tiny tragedy of an unpaired sock. He looked for its mate between the sofa cushions and on the floor but couldn't find it anywhere. This gave him a little bit of a bad feeling even in the midst of his relief and gladness. There was something disturbing and sorrowful about an unpaired sock and everybody knew it was a lousy omen. He resolved to keep his misgivings to himself.

Meanwhile, the cat had wandered off yet again.

This time she had a good reason for doing it. She was puzzled. Her world was out of whack. Nothing was like it usually was at this hour of the night. The house felt empty but the doors were open and the lights were on in the backyard and the kitchen. There were dirty dishes abandoned in the sink as they'd never been before, and there'd been no one standing at the counter to arrange things just perfectly so she could take a cool drink directly from the faucet.

Confused, miffed as only cats can be, she went upstairs in search of some comforting familiarity. But the big bed where her people slept, and that always afforded her a choice of delicious canyons between feet and shins to nestle in, was empty. In the other room, there was no trace of the recent visitor whose warm aroma reminded her of French fries.

She meowed once into the vacancy, paused for a moment on the landing, then went downstairs again and out through the open door to the backyard, where she skirted the miniature swimming pool and found the break in the foliage that was her portal to the world beyond. She slunk through narrow streets and padded straight across the cemetery that human beings had to drive around, always weaving but always heading toward the briny smell of the ocean. When she reached the promenade, she jumped up onto the seawall and, making her way along the top of it, more confident and lithe than any gymnast, she came at last to the spot where the hot dog truck had used to be, and where now there stood a big black car with two large men leaning back against the hood.

22

"What happened to your head?" asked Bert the Shirt.

It was after eleven by then. Meg and Peter, rattled by their parley at the hot dog, had rung the doorbell and were standing at the threshold, Peter looking like a Civil War re-enacter who had wandered off the battlefield with a bloody strip of white rag tied just above his ears and dangling down his neck. "Oh, nothing much," he said. "I just got scalped by a machete."

"Grazed," his wife corrected. "Nicked. It was an accident. Our friends thought we were Mafia thugs coming after them. No offense, Bert."

"None taken. Come in, come in." To Peter, he said, "You want some iodine for that? A Band-Aid maybe?"

"Band-Aid? Bert, I practically got my head cut off."

"He likes the bandage," Meg put in. "You know, that red badge of courage kind of thing."

To no one in particular, Peter said, "Great, I've probably got sepsis, she's making obscure references to a book nobody reads."

They stepped into the living room, where Sonny was sitting with Nacho next to the neat piles of clean clothes. Meg said, "Sorry we couldn't tell you sooner, Sonny. We just couldn't."

"I understand. No hard feelin's. How's the cat?"

"Safe at home," said Peter, incorrectly. "And gradually getting over you."

Sonny just nodded and petted the dog that also adored him.

Bert invited the new visitors to sit, though he couldn't help noticing with some slight unease that they had nothing in their hands. He said, "Well, I thought we'd toast wit' some Prosecco, but maybe better to do it, ya know, after we finish up our little bit a business wit' the murderers outside. So, d'ya leave the package inna car or what?"

Peter was perched on the very edge of a threadbare chair. He said, "Well, um, we need to talk about that."

"What's to talk?" said Sonny.

Meg said simply, "There is no package."

"No package?" the big man blurted. "But there has to be a package!"

"Well, there isn't," Peter said.

"I can't believe this. Did your knucklehead friends even look for it? I can tell you exactly where it is."

"Where it was," corrected Meg. "It was in a metal drawer with a bunch of moldy buns and rotten sauerkraut and rancid relish, and our friends were tidying up so they wouldn't get rats, so they took out all that stuff and burned it."

"Burned it?" Bert said very softly.

"Burned it," Peter confirmed. "They even showed us the

place they did it. Nothing left but a circle of ashes on the ground."

In an almost pleading voice, Sonny said, "But the package—"

"Look," said Meg, "they meant no harm. How were they supposed to know it was important? It was just thrown in there with the other garbage."

Sonny's face was flushed and his fists were balled against the sofa cushion. "Well, if they hadn't'a stole the fuckin' hot dog inna first place—"

"Which, as things stand, is neither here nor there," Bert put in quietly, "so let's not argue. I mean, ya can drive yourself crazy wit' the what ifs. What if the buns weren't moldy? What if the relish wasn't rotten? Point is, it is what it is, and what it is, is that midnight's just arounda corner and Livingstone's package is toasted onna ground, which is to say, we got a big fuckin' problem, pardon my French."

"So what the hell we gonna do, Bert?" asked the big man.

By reflex, the old man reached down to scratch his dog between the ears, but the dog was on the sofa next to Sonny. So he just said, "Well, for starters, I suggest we open up a bottle a Prosecco and consider our options, stinkin' though they are."

It was 11:30 and Frankie Citarella was looking in his rear-view mirror as he pulled out of the parking lot of the Flagler House Hotel.

The black SUV, with its two big men up front and dapper silhouette in back, was still behind him, as it had been all evening, as patient and tireless as a guilty conscience. It had tailed him during his half-hearted effort to follow the rangy and unhelpful man from the public shower. It had lingered behind him during the precious hours he'd wasted checking out the trailer parks of Stock Island and Big Coppitt in an increasingly frantic but futile search for the pilfered wagon. It had followed him down dusty roads that dead-ended at defunct marinas or at abandoned construction sites; and, just minutes before, it had trailed him to the *porte cochere* of the Flagler House when he'd stopped there to have what proved to be a radically brief but very painful conversation with his wife.

He'd gone up to what had been their room with the honest intention of being nice. He was feeling awfully sorry for himself, and therefore sentimental, and he wanted to say something conciliatory, maybe even something tender, something she could fondly remember him by if things turned out as badly as it seemed they would. But somehow the moment went terribly wrong.

He'd gone into the room, which seemed at first to be vacant. But then he heard soft music from the direction of the bathroom. He listened for some seconds then pushed open the door behind which his wife was sitting in a bubble bath with suds up to her shoulders, smoothing her nails with an emery board, and smiling and singing to herself. For a few heartbeats he just stared at her with something like affection, but gradually a feeling grew in him that swamped any chance he might have had of saying something pleasant. He was galled that she seemed so utterly content after a day without him, humiliated and furious that she could be so blithe and breezy while they were on the outs. How long had it been since he'd seen her so relaxed? How many months since he'd heard her sing? Had their marriage really turned that lousy?

Caught between rage and a sudden shameful urge to cry, all he could manage to say was, "What the hell are you so goddamn happy about?"

He slammed the bathroom door without waiting for an answer and went downstairs again.

The black SUV fell in behind him as he left the parking lot and drove with no real hope to the place along the promenade where the hot dog wagon used to be, and where now a Burmese cat was behaving very strangely.

23

"Honesty's the best policy," the old man was saying. "'Specially when ya can't thinka nothin' better. I mean, what else we gonna tell the guy? Besides, we kinda kept up our parta the bargain. He said we had till midnight to find his package. Well, we found it. Sorta. I mean, it's burned to a crisp but he can't say we didn't find it. So maybe, just as a possibility, we just level wit' 'im and ask for mercy."

"He didn't strike me as the merciful type," said Sonny.

"No, not offhand," admitted Bert.

Meg said, "Confucius taught that showing mercy is the highest privilege of the powerful."

"Great," said Peter, adjusting the angle of his now scabbed bandage. "I'm sure this butcher reads Confucius all the time."

Sonny got up from the sofa, paced a zig-zag lap through the cluttered living room, then posted himself at the window, plucked the miniature binoculars from the sill, and peered out, panning up and down the beach. With an odd detachment, like a foreign correspondent reporting from a cozy bunker on the troubles of some faraway stranger rather than on his own, he mildly announced that Citarella had just pulled in across the street and that Livingstone's SUV was parking close behind him. He confirmed that several car doors were swinging open and people climbing out. Then he paused, and twisted the little dials of the glasses, and leaned in closer to the window, and squinted through the lenses, and said, "But hold on a second. That's your cat. Your cat's down there."

"My Sasha?" exclaimed Peter, leaping to his feet.

"Yeah, jumpin' back and forth between the seawall and the curb. Right in the middle of everything."

"Down there with those assassins? Let me see!" He wrestled the binocs away from the big man and focused them with trembling fingers. The cat looked very small and fragile as it slunk among the beefy thugs and hulking vehicles. One glance was all it took to make his mind up. "I'm going down to get her."

He bolted toward the door, Meg right alongside.

Bert said, "Hey, wait a sec, we ain't decided on our story yet."

"But it's my cat!" said Peter, as though there were simply nothing more to consider.

"Right, and these guys don't mess around and you two really ain't involved so far. Might be healthier to keep it that way."

Peter didn't answer, just reached for the doorknob, his bandage streaming out behind him.

Bert looked at Sonny. Sonny looked at Bert. There was no time to come to a decision, and there was no decision to be made. There was only one right thing they could do. The old man struggled to his feet with Nacho in his arms and they all trundled together out into the hallway and down onto the street.

⚓ ⚓ ⚓

Pineapple and Fred were sleeping on the ground. Or trying to. Piney wouldn't let himself enjoy the comfort of the hot dog just then. He felt too guilty about the deadly trouble they were causing Sonny, and even guiltier about burning up the package that could have saved his life; way too guilty to fall asleep. He rolled over for the tenth time in the last couple minutes and spoke across the remains of the campfire to Fred. "We just never should've taken the wagon."

Fred was feeling guilty, too, though it would not have been his style to admit it. "Hey," he said, "we been through this. How could we have known?"

"Well, I guess we couldn't. But maybe that's a good reason not to take something that isn't yours. If you don't know where it's gonna lead, I mean."

"Water under the bridge, my friend."

Mosquitoes buzzed in the two men's ears. Fred swatted at them. Piney left them alone. He felt like maybe he deserved to be bitten. "I should've been more careful when I burned the stuff."

"You were careful, Piney. You broke it into little piles."

"Maybe I should've gone slower."

"How much slower could a person go?"

"I dunno. I just feel bad about it. Like there was something I should've noticed but I didn't. To me, it was all just stuff that needed burning. Light a match, ten minutes later all you got's a pile of ashes and some shiny gravel. And then to think this is what Sonny's life, maybe anybody's life, comes down to. Some ashes and some gravel. Kinda spooky if you think about it."

"So don't," Fred advised. "Look, you tried your best."

Pineapple gave an unconvinced shrug and looked up at the positions of the misted stars. "Must be close to midnight."

"Yeah, I guess it is."

"Hope we don't hear any shots or anything."

"Maybe the guy's bluffing. Maybe Sonny got away somewhere. Come on, Piney, let's try and get some sleep."

⚓ ⚓ ⚓

"Um, excuse me," said Peter, as he gingerly stepped between the big black SUVS and past the cringing form of Frankie Citarella and through the knot of Livingstone's bulky men now standing with their thick arms crossed and their feet as firmly planted as those of Sumo wrestlers. "I'd just like to get my cat."

This drew some annoyed and puzzled glances, though at first no one said a word or tried to interfere. But the cat didn't seem to want to be rescued. When Peter approached her at the seawall, she jumped down onto the promenade. When he tried to scoop her from the sidewalk, she slunk off to the curb. Still pursuing, knees bent, torso folded at the waist, he kept saying in a singsong voice, "Come on, pretty kitty. No time to be temperamental."

After yet another unsuccessful lunge and grab, the thugs finally lost patience. One of them said, "Listen, buddy, we got business here. Cat or no cat, you need to get lost."

"Look, it'll just take one more sec—"

The plea got no farther, because by then Meg and Sonny and Bert and Nacho were halfway across the road, and the thugs, apparently uneasy at the numbers and momentum of the growing crowd, had quickly and invisibly pulled pistols from their waistbands and were holding them chest-high at the ready.

"That's close enough!" barked one of them, though at the sight of the guns, the visitors had already stopped stone cold in awkward and unbalanced poses, as in a game of freeze tag or a stuck frame of film when the projector suddenly breaks down.

By reflex, Bert raised the arm that wasn't cradling the dog. "Look, guys," he said calmly, "don't get crazy. We ain't packin'. We just need to talk wit' Livingstone."

The thug waited for the boss to tap on the window glass before he answered. Then he said, "Okay, but no fast movements."

The old man said, "Do I look fast to you?"

The cat meowed. Peter spread his arms and made one more swooping move toward it. A thug said, "Stay the fuck still or I'll shoot the goddamn cat." Peter froze in a posture reminiscent of Al Jolson.

A back window of the lead SUV silently slid open. Behind it, Livingstone was dapper as ever in his perfect hat and shades. He turned a brief, dismissive glance at Sonny and at Citarella and said, "Glad to see you boys keep some of your appointments, at least. Saves the trouble of chasing you down."

Bert said, "Which, inna final analysis and after we acquaint ya wit' some important information or you might say new developments which touch upon and are even of the essence of our problem, we hope and at least slightly trust would not be necessary or even called for anyway. So can we talk?"

The dapper man shot back his shirt cuff and looked down at his Rolex. "Sure. Talk all you want. It's ten of twelve."

Sasha meowed again and moved a few steps up the curb. Peter tried to catch her eye to beg her to stay still but the cat would not look back. His leg began to cramp from holding his absurd position.

"S'okay," said Bert. "Let's revisit the unfortunate events that have brought us to what I guess would usually be called this critical junction. First, a shipment a somethin' that none of us knows what the hell it is went sadly awry or ya could even say astray, but whose fault it was or who should bear the onus or the blame for this unfortunate screw-up remains shrouded in doubt and it would not be amiss to call it, whaddyacallit, ambiguity."

Livingstone looked at his watch again.

Bert said, "And meanwhile, as we stand here innee eye a the storm, so to speak—"

At that, Meg, who'd been taking measured yoga breaths, just couldn't stand it anymore and broke in with her usual directness. "And meanwhile, Mr. Livingstone, we found your package."

The dapper man leaned just slightly forward; for him, it was an effusive gesture. "You did?"

"We did."

"So you have it?"

"We don't."

Livingstone's jaw tightened down. The sound of his teeth grinding could be heard in the street. "Are you playing games with me, Miss? I really don't like games."

"It's the truth. We found the package. What's left of it. It's been destroyed. It was an accident."

"An accident," mulled Livingstone in a murderously quiet voice. "What kind of accident?"

"It was burned."

"And how the hell you know all this?" Citarella blurted out.

A thug smacked him in the mouth and told him to shut up. He held his cut lip and glared at Sonny like even the slap was his fault.

Livingstone resumed with a single quiet word. "Where?"

"What's the difference where?"

"Where'd it happen, lady? I need to know."

Meg said nothing.

Peter, from his absurd stage-bow position, said, "Look, it doesn't matter where. And there are innocent people—"

"Are there?" interrupted Livingstone. "Really? Innocent people? What a quaint idea. Listen, no one's innocent. Now where the hell's my package?"

A long mute moment passed. Meg gazed straight ahead. Peter looked down at the pavement. Bert stroked Nacho to ease his squirming. Citarella and Sonny stared past one another.

Livingstone gnashed his teeth. Then, in his soft and clenched and sentencing voice, he said abruptly, "That's it.

Enough. Grab the woman. Throw her in the car."

A thug lurched forward, grabbed Meg's wrist, and wrenched her arm behind her back. She winced but made no sound.

Peter rose from his crouch and shouted, "You take your hands off her!"

The thug smirked and kept to his orders.

"Grab the cat-man too," instructed Livingstone. "Take all of them. It's almost midnight. We find my shipment or they die."

For some seconds there was a blur of prodding and poking, Sonny shielding Bert as they were shoved headfirst into the car, Peter scrambling across knees and elbows as he tried to get closer to his wife. Then, suddenly, the chaos was finished, doors were slammed, and the street was empty...except for Sasha, who serenely jogged along the curb in the direction of the airport as if pointing the way for the jam-packed SUV's.

24

Fred's machete lay beside him on the ground, and he reached for it by habit at the first sound of vehicles plunking off the paved road and onto the scrub-and-coral shoulder that led to the narrow pathway to the clearing. But as the noise grew closer and bigger and more enveloping—foliage being bashed and battered, rocks clawing at undercarriages, engines revving from an angry growl to a whining roar—he realized the weapon would be useless; he let it drop and stood unarmed in the ghostly glow of the faded fire. As branches snapped and saplings were obliterated, Pineapple clambered to his feet. "Spend my whole life trying to stay out of trouble," he muttered. "Still just couldn't get it right. "

The engine roar grew deafening. Bouncing beams of headlights raked across the clearing, piercing the darkness like klieg lights at a premiere, sometimes finding puzzled moths in empty space, sometimes lighting up the service window of the hot dog as if it were a puppet stage. When the SUV's finally smashed their way free of the woods and stood idling, as if panting, at the edge of the open ground, the brightness was like the flash of an explosion.

Car doors opened. Four men with guns spilled out.

Sonny helped Bert and Nacho take the long step down to the stony ground. Peter and Meg held hands, his bandage twisted and askew, her gaze distant but steady. Citarella, standing alone, made a disdainful gesture toward the hot dog and said, "Fucking thing was right there the whole time? Like half a mile from where it started? And this fucking loser couldn't find it?"

Sonny said, "You didn't find it either, Frankie."

Bert stroked his dog and added, "Too busy talkin' trash about your wife."

A man with a gun told them all to shut up.

There was a brief, still moment, then Livingstone emerged from his car, the tilt of his wide-brimmed hat perfect as ever and his sunglasses in place even at midnight. With the glare behind him and the darkness in front, he looked less like a silhouette than a walking shadow, a solid absence. Slowly, he walked toward Fred and Piney. Even the frogs and crickets went silent at his approach. Very softly, he said, "I understand there's been a so-called accident. I believe one of you burned something that belongs to me."

Peter called out, "Look, he didn't know."

Livingstone ignored the comment. "Which one of you did it?"

Piney's knees were locked and his arms felt dead at his sides, but there was no hesitation in his answer. "It was me. I did it. Fred here had nothing to do with it."

"Where was the fire?"

"Where?"

"Where. Exactly. Show me."

Piney managed to take a couple of steps and to lift a

trembling finger to point out the faded ring of ash in the penumbra between the headlights and the darkness.

Looking back over his shoulder, Livingstone said just two words to his crew, "Find them."

At the bewildering order, two of his men put their guns away, strode over to the ring of ashes, eased down onto their knees, and started combing through the cinders with their fingers. A low fog of burned dust rose up around them. Smears of oily ash stained their pants and shoes. The acrid smell of stale smoke filled the clearing. Nacho sneezed. Weirdly, avidly, the two men pawed the ground and sifted, crawling along like crabs until they had covered the breadth and width of Piney's bonfire and let all the ashes slip between their fingers. Then they looked up at their boss and shook their heads.

Livingstone gnashed his teeth, took one slow step toward Pineapple, and backhanded him across the cheek. "You're lying."

Piney barely flinched. "No sir, I'm not. I swear. Whatever was in the hot dog, I burned it."

Fred said, "It's true, Mister. I saw it all laid out. Whatever was in there, it went in the fire."

The dapper man considered that a moment, then wheeled around toward the others. His gaze flicking back and forth between Sonny and Citarella, he said, "All right then. Let's do some simple logic. Either these two nobodies are lying, or the package wasn't where it was supposed to be. Which is it?"

"Look," said Sonny, "I put that shipment where it was supposed to go, then I closed up shop like Citarella told me to. That's the God's honest truth."

"No it ain't," claimed Citarella. "You left too soon. You bolted."

Seemingly as much in sorrow as in anger, Livingstone shook his head and spoke in the general direction of Meg and Peter. "You see, so much for your quaint idea about innocent people. Someone's lying here. Or blaming someone else. Or making lame excuses. They're all just different kinds of lies. Too damn many lies and too damn many liars in the world. Too damn many witnesses, too."

To his men, in a casual, offhand voice, he said, "Go ahead and line them up. We've wasted enough time here."

The thugs who'd scrabbled through the cinders had dusted themselves off and taken out their guns again. They herded Fred and Piney into the pool of brightness where the others stood. Bert was clutching Nacho to his shrunken chest. Peter and Meg squeezed their hands together; with her free hand, she took Sonny's. Citarella had no one to hold on to.

"I'm almost sorry to do this," said the dapper man. "Maybe not that sorry."

He gave the killers a nod and they raised their pistols in nearly perfect sync.

Bert covered the dog's eyes with his papery hand. Then he said, "'Scuse me, Livingstone, no hard feelin's here. I unnerstand you're gonna do what ya gotta do, but could I please ask for one small courtesy as a whaddyacallit, a prerogative of my advancin' years, which don't seem likely t'advance much further, namely, since it doesn't look like it's gonna matter a damn, why go down wonderin'? So can I please ask just as a matter a natural curiosity, what the hell your guys were diggin' inna dirt for and that's causin' all this trouble?"

Livingstone frowned at that, then almost smiled. Suddenly he seemed almost relaxed. His decision had been made. His assassins had their weapons ready. His victims were quailing in front of him. He was almost enjoying the moment. He said, "Why not, old man? You seem to like guessing games. You seem to like hints. Let's see how many hints it takes you. My product comes from Africa. People die procuring it. Yet the product itself is almost indestructible. It can't be scratched. It can't be burned—"

"Diamonds," said Meg.

"Very good. The lady gets the gold star. Diamonds. In the rough. Uncut, unpolished, lifted at enormous risk from the fields of Angola and Botswana, smuggled past the guards with their Uzi's and their dogs, and on their way to the cutters in New York, who'll pay a fortune for their quality and size. So now you know. You won't die wondering. Feel better?"

Slides were pumped and bullets clicked into their chambers.

Piney said, "Could you please wait one more second? I was wondering. I got a question. In the rough, you said. So, not polished or anything? So, like, they might just look like shiny gravel? Like regular old gravel, maybe, like the gravel you see every day, but got burned and turned shiny in the fire?"

"To an uneducated eye," said Livingstone, "yes, they might almost look like shiny gravel."

"Gee, that's really interesting," said Pineapple.

"Why?" said Livingstone. "Why's it interesting to you? You seen any gravel like that?"

Piney shrugged like it was no big deal. "Yeah. A bunch.

All different sizes and shapes. I thought they were really pretty. Some were kind of yellow, some more to the blue. I picked 'em up soon as the fire cooled. Put 'em over there in the tip jar."

He gestured toward the counter at the service window of the hot dog, where a mayonnaise jar full of rough diamonds glinted dully in the glare from the headlights.

All eyes turned. A thug brought the jar to Livingstone. He held it up to the light, gave it a shake like a maraca, and saw faint fire twinkling deep inside the stones. He almost smiled.

Guns were lowered, long-held breaths were released, and at that moment a Burmese cat jogged into the clearing, rubbed its flank against Sonny's leg, then meowed and jumped up into Peter's arms.

EPILOGUE

Well, Pineapple here, to say I guess that about wraps it up. Like I said at the start, it's a strange story but sort of normal for where it happened. Key West just has a lot of crazy stories, and I really don't know why. Are people crazier here than in other places? I don't know, but my guess is that people are crazy everywhere. Maybe they just don't keep it bottled up as much down here. Maybe they don't feel they need to, what with all the coming and going and all the different types of people passing through for different reasons and chasing different things. And maybe that's a good thing. Not to keep it bottled up, I mean. Why hold the craziness inside and let it make you even crazier? Anyway, what you sometimes end up with is a story that you can hardly believe it really happened, but at the same time it just doesn't seem like anyone could make it up. So, if you don't think anyone could make it up, but you have your doubts about whether it really happened, where does that leave you? I wonder about that sometimes. Then again, I wonder about a lot of stuff. Why not? Wondering doesn't cost money and every now and then you can actually figure something out.

Anyway, if you liked the story and you're curious at all about what's been going on with some of us since that sort of hairy moment in the clearing, there's at least a little bit I can tell you.

First of all, Livingstone and his helpers pretty much lost interest in us as soon as they got their gravel back. They took the tip jar, got back in their cars, slammed their way out through the torn up mangroves, and left us standing there in the dark, pretty shook up but glad to be alive. I'm pretty sure they had a plane waiting to take them back to Africa. The reason I'm pretty sure is that, just a little while after they left us, there was a helluva roar and rattle as a jet took off, and it was at a time when the airport was supposedly all closed down and there weren't any flights. So I think it must've been them. Bert seemed to think so, too, because when the jet went over I heard him say, "Bon voyage, assholes."

As for Frankie Citarella, the wiry guy with the money clip who'd sort of made himself the odd man out, which I'm guessing is the story of his life because he just wasn't straight with people and was always sneaking around and trying to take advantage, what I heard is that he left Key West the very next day, but without his wife. That part gets sort of interesting, and I'll get to it in a minute.

The rest of us, I'm happy to say, have all stayed friends. I guess there's something about standing shoulder to shoulder in front of a firing squad and coming within a few seconds of getting your head blown off that makes you feel sort of close to people. Anyway, a few days after that happened, Peter stopped by the hot dog and invited me and Fred to a little party at their house. Actually, what he said was that Meg wanted to have a ritual gathering of gratitude, or something close to that, but what I made of it was party, and to be honest, this made me pretty nervous. It might sound weird to a lot of folks, but I don't think I'd ever in my life been invited to a party at someone's actual house. Kids' birthdays, maybe, long, long time ago. Or stuff at churches and shelters and such. But at someone's house? Never. So I was afraid I'd do something wrong or not know how to act.

As it turned out, the party was very nice and easy. I got to go in the pool. True, it didn't have a diving board, but it was a hot day and it felt great to have the sun on my back while my legs were cool and I didn't have to worry about stepping on sharp coral or having slimy things swim over my feet. Meg was sitting right opposite me in the shade of an umbrella and she started telling me about Buddhism. There were some fancy words involved, but basically it turned out to be a lot of the same stuff I've been doing all along. Try to stay calm. Don't kill things if you can help it. Don't get too wrapped up with stuff or things you can't fix anyway. I mean, it all made perfect sense to me. So who knew I was a Buddhist all these years? Then again, maybe part of being Buddhist is not even noticing you're Buddhist.

Anyway, there were some nice snacks and Peter was pouring wine, which Fred didn't seem to realize or care has a lot more alcohol than beer. So he got pretty looped but there was no one looking for an argument or anything to get all worked up about, so no harm came of it. Sonny was there with Citarella's wife, though I think it's fair to say she wasn't Citarella's wife anymore, except officially. Her name was Cecile, and those two just seemed crazy about each other. She kept touching his arm. He kept touching her knee. They looked at each other like no one else was there. Now and then they'd giggle. I still don't know what they were giggling about. I guess when you're that crazy about someone there's a lot of private jokes.

Bert was there with Nacho, and they were wearing matching outfits. Me, I'm not much for clothes, but I have to say that man can dress, and so can his dog. Bert was wearing green pants and a bright yellow shirt and reminded me a little of a double-stick lemon-lime ice pop. I mean, not exactly, but you get the picture. The dog had a jacket that was the same bright yellow except it ended in green cuffs. I'd never seen a dog with cuffs and I wondered how Bert got it to stay still long enough to get it dressed. Then again, maybe the dog's favorite thing was getting all dolled up for a party. That's not anything I know about.

Anyway, Bert held the dog in his lap for awhile, then put it down on the pool deck so it could go over and play with Meg and Peter's cat, which had been hanging around the whole time right under Peter's lounge chair. The dog and the cat sniffed each other and pawed the air like they were having a pretend boxing match, and everybody watched because, let's face it, how can you not? Then the cat suddenly lost interest, rolled over, and yawned.

Bert said, "And right there's the difference between a dog and a cat. Wit' a dog, if it's playin' a game it likes, it'll play it all day long. It'll play it till the cows come home. Wit' a cat, even if it's havin' fun, it'll just quit all of a sudden and get this attitude like, okay, now I'm bored, go away. And the dog is, like, *Wha'd I do wrong?* And the cat is, like, *Why even talk about it? You'll never unnerstand.*"

"True, cats are complicated," said Peter, whose hair, I should mention, was mostly grown back on the bald spot where Fred had accidentally shaved him with the machete. Then he admitted right there in front of everyone how much it hurt his feelings when Sasha was ignoring him and only seemed to care for Sonny. Sonny told him not to take it personal, animals just seemed to like him. But Meg thought it was much more that. She thought Sasha had been mad at Peter because Burmese cats have special powers, and the cat realized that the reason Sonny was in trouble was because

Peter wouldn't tell anyone where the hot dog was. Fred, who wasn't following things that clearly by then, said he had a question, and asked Meg if Burmese and Buddhist meant the same thing. Meg said not necessarily.

Anyway, this back and forth about whether cats have special powers opened up the question of whether the cat could really have found the hot dog by sense of smell and whether she was trying to lead people to it to get the whole mess figured out. Everyone had a different opinion about this. Except me. I had no opinion. I guess my feeling was she's a cat, I'm not a cat, so how the heck should I know? But at the same time, I felt a little bad that I didn't have an opinion, like I wasn't holding up my end of the bargain. Everyone except me just seemed to get it that if you go to a party, you're supposed to have opinions on whatever might come up, whether you know anything about it or not. I'll try to do better on this in case I ever get invited to another party.

Anyway, at some point we pretty well wore out the stuff about the cat, and the talking came around to what Sonny was gonna do now that he wasn't in trouble anymore. Cecile picked the ball up and ran with it on that one, saying right away that he wouldn't be going back to the life he'd had before because it didn't suit him anyway and who cared about the stupid money and he was too good a person to be dragged through the mud by the Frankie Citarellas of this world. Or something close to that is what she said. So that cleared it up about what he wasn't gonna do. When he finally got the chance to talk about what he was gonna do, he got a sort of faraway little smile on his face and said, "Ya know, not countin' when I'm right next to Cecile, I don't think I was ever happier than when I was cookin' dogs and fries for people. Honest work where I knew what I was doin'. Slingin' sauerkraut. Fillin' up the mustard jars. Talkin' to customers, makin' 'em happy. No stress, no complications. I don't think I'd mind just doin' that again."

Well, when he said that, I looked at Fred. Fred looked at me. I'm pretty sure we were thinking the exact same thing, which was that if Sonny wanted the wagon back and could get the axle fixed to move it, well, fair enough, it was his. That's life. Don't plan on hanging on to something just because you have it at the moment.

So I was thinking this, trying not to let it show that I was a little bit upset, which, Buddhist or no Buddhist, is only human after all, when Bert suddenly said, "So whaddya say we open a little hot dog joint downtown?"

Nobody knew exactly what to say to that, so everyone stayed quiet while the old man gestured to the dog, and the dog ran over and jumped into his lap, and he scratched it between the ears and then went on. "Why not? I got a little money set aside that's not doin' me any good. You know the hot dog business. We got some friends who maybe could use a job. Me, I wouldn't mind havin' a new hangout. What say we find a little place not too far off Duval and open up a shop?"

Well, to make a long story short, that's pretty much what happened. Somehow or other, Sonny and Cecile found a doughnut place down on Fleming that was going out of business, and Bert fronted them some cash, and they turned it into a hot dog joint where the two of them could work side by side in matching paper hats. They were nice enough to offer jobs to Fred and me, and we partway took them up on it. Fred is not what you'd call a full-time or on-the-books type of guy, but he put in a couple weeks' demolition work when they were ripping out the doughnut stuff, and that caught us up on money for awhile. They offered me a counter job, but I didn't think I could hack it having to talk to customers and make change and keep orders straight. Maybe I could've done it, who knows, but it would've made me awfully nervous. Anyway, what I do instead is go in a couple of nights a week to help with clean-up. I get a few dollars and all the hot dogs I want, which is quite a few after the long walk down the promenade to downtown.

So, all in all, I guess you could say that everything is back to normal. The Kaplans got their car fixed up. I walk past their house sometimes when I'm on my way to work. I don't ring the bell or anything because I don't want to bother them, but sometimes if they're out on the porch, we visit for a while. Peter usually seems worried about something, but the something that he's worried about is different every time. I guess some people just like to worry for the sake of worrying, and what the worrying is about is sort of a separate question. Who knows? I don't really understand it.

As for me and Fred, I'm happy to say we're still living in the hot dog and that we have it fixed up pretty nice, with a little propane fridge and a two-burner cooktop. But cozy as it is, we still sleep outside most nights when the weather's good, and we still usually make a campfire even if it's not for cooking. It just feels right. Sometimes we talk about the crazy night with the diamonds, and Fred says I was the hero. I just laugh when he says that. I know I wasn't. Heroes do big things, brave things. What the heck did I do? All I did was get curious about gravel and wonder about it and notice that not all gravel is the same and that some of it is shiny. Not exactly Superman stuff. Still, I'm glad I noticed. Then again, it's not like I could've helped myself from wondering about gravel after looking at it all day long. That's just the way I am, I guess. Some people worry for the sake of worrying. I wonder for the sake of wondering. Usually it gets me nowhere, and I'm totally okay with that. I mean, where am I trying to go with it? Then again, if it happens to come in handy once or twice in life, I guess you could just say that's a bonus.

ABOUT THE AUTHOR

Laurence Shames is the author of sixteen *Key West Capers,* as well as many other works of fiction and nonfiction. As a ghostwriter, he has penned four *New York Times* bestsellers, in four different categories, under four different names. Formerly a columnist for *Esquire* and *The New York Observer,* he has contributed hundreds of articles and essays to publications including *Vanity Fair, Outside, Travel & Leisure,* and *The New York Times Magazine.* His work has been translated into more than a dozen languages, and he is a recipient of the United Kingdom's *Macallan Last Laugh Dagger* for his comic mystery writing.

To learn more, please visit https://laurenceshames.com

Works by Laurence Shames

Key West Capers—
>The Paradise Gig
>Nacho Unleashed
>One Big Joke
>One Strange Date
>Key West Luck
>Tropical Swap
>Shot on Location
>The Naked Detective
>Welcome to Paradise
>Mangrove Squeeze
>Virgin Heat
>Tropical Depression
>Sunburn
>Scavenger Reef
>Florida Straits

Key West Short Fiction—
>Chickens

New York & California Novels—
>Money Talks
>The Angels' Share

Nonfiction—
>The Hunger for More
>The Big Time

Printed in Great Britain
by Amazon

37251239R00118